SECRET OF THE SILVER ECLIPSE

A ROTHAR & LEENA ADVENTURE
JP WILDER

EDGE WEAVER LLC

Secret of the Silver Eclipse
A Lothar and Leena Adventure

Edge Weaver Realms is an imprint of Edge Weaver LLC

Book Design: Marie Ito

Kindle ISBN: 978-1-964406-57-2

Paperback ISBN: 978-1-964406-93-0

Published in the United States of America

Edge Weaver LLC
19360 Rinaldi #681
Porter Ranch, CA 91326-1607

CONTENTS

CHAPTER 1: A JOB IN SHADOWS

Rothar sat in the back corner of the Iron Stag, his fingers tracing the rim of the half-empty mug of ale, eyes shifting over the room like a hawk surveying its hunting ground. The tavern roared with life: the scrape of chairs, the bawdy laughter of men who had seen too much blood and too few rewards, and the whisper of private deals struck in dark corners. A haze of smoke hovered thickly, clinging to the air like a possessive wraith, mixing with the tang of spilled ale and the sharp, metallic scent of sweat and old

iron. It was a place where ambition and desperation shared a drink, and Rothar fit in seamlessly.

He noted every detail—the flicker of a dagger
at a mercenary's belt, the wary glance from a
cloaked figure near the door, the subtle movement of hands hidden under tables, exchang-
ing coin or something far more sinister. Habit
kept him alert; instincts honed as a soldier and
tempered in HollowGate's brutal back alleys kept
him alive.

A table away, a boisterous argument erupted, chairs scraping harshly as a burly sellsword
lunged to his feet, tankard sloshing ale down
his front. Rothar's eyes flicked over the scene,
his muscles tensing before dismissing the threat.
Just another dispute over honor or women, or
the last round paid for with stolen coin. The Stag
attracted such people like flies to rot.

He wasn't there to drink, at least not in peace.
He was waiting.

And she was late.

The tavern door banged open, and the sharp,
bitter HollowGate wind coming off the great in-
ner sea known as the Dark Water cut through the

warmth inside. The noise dimmed for a heartbeat as a tall, lithe figure paused in the entrance, framed by the sickly glow of lanterns that sputtered against the night. A surge of cold followed her, carrying the acrid bite of city smoke and rain-soaked grime.

Leena.

She stood in the threshold as if commanding a stage, arms wide and head held high. Her platinum hair, pulled back into a severe braid, shimmered like polished silver, catching the low light. Her dark surcoat hugged her body, the fabric taut over toned limbs that spoke of agility and untapped power. The cloak pinned at her throat swept out behind her like a living shadow, her sorcerer's wand tucked dangerously in her belt, and charms chimed softly on her wrists—a warning as much as an adornment.

Rothar's jaw tightened, half in admiration, half in annoyance. She enjoyed the attention far too much. The room, full of hard men and sharper women, seemed to shift in her direction, curious, hungry. Even the sellsword, mid-argument, paused to take her in, eyes narrowing with interest. Leena reveled in it, a slight smirk touching her full lips as she sauntered through the crowd with a sway that was deliberate, each step echoing confidence.

When her gaze found Rothar's, her smile widened, the glint in her eyes daring him to chastise her for the spectacle. She glided to the table and dropped into the chair opposite him, crossing her legs with an elegance that belied the iron coiled beneath her surface.

"You're late," Rothar said, his voice low, more statement than rebuke.

Leena's hand shot out before he could react, snagging his mug and taking a long pull. She set it down with a flourish and a satisfied exhale. "Traffic," she said, unbothered that it was a lie. "The streets are crawling tonight. You know how it is."

He scowled, reclaiming the mug and watching her through narrowed eyes. Her charm bracelets glinted as she adjusted her cloak, the tiny runes on them catching the lamplight with a dangerous gleam. "More likely you were entertaining some fool with coin in his pocket."

A mischievous grin tugged at her lips. "Why not both? Time's a precious commodity in HollowGate." Her gaze softened, growing serious as she leaned in, voice dropping so only he could hear. "And tonight, I've got something more valuable than coin."

Rothar's brow lifted, the casual drink momentarily forgotten. "A job?"

She produced a folded piece of parchment from inside her surcoat, placing it between them with a deliberate motion. "A noblewoman's—some Lady Velora—has gone missing . . . or something. The Silver Eclipse wants it handled discreetly."

The murmur of the tavern receded, drowned out by the sudden rush of blood in Rothar's ears. His fingers brushed the coarse paper, but he did not open it yet. His eyes flicked to hers, searching for the trap. "Or something . . ." Rothar laughed and drew a nasty look from his companion. "Of course. The Eclipse? Why us? They've their own men, trained better and paid more."

"Who's the broker? Was it—"

"Yes, Kaelira." Leena's eyes sparkled, and for a moment, Rothar could almost see the fire beneath the ice of her exterior.

Rothar groaned.

Leena continued, "they don't want the guard involved. Questions lead to answers, and the Eclipse prefers shadows over light."

He nodded slowly. The aristocracy of Hollow-Gate, particularly the Silver Eclipse, was a nest of power and poison, led by the Grand Mayor, Lady Elira Voss—a shadowy figure people didn't cross. the Eclipse dealt in secrets and whispered threats that broke a man with no need to shed blood. Taking a job from them was like putting a serpent in your pocket—warm now, but deadly when it turned.

"Tell me," he said, folding his arms, "why should we be the ones stepping into their lair, finding their lost kitten, and risk losing our heads?"

Leena's lips curved in a smile that could have melted iron. "Because they're desperate. And desperation pays well. Besides, a favor from the

Eclipse could be worth more than any sack of gold."

Rothar's eyes darkened, the specter of past dealings with HollowGate's nobility, and visions of Leena being stretched over the breaking wheel if they failed, haunting the edges of his mind. He reached for the parchment and paused, weighing it as if it were a blade that might cut him. "And what makes you think this won't end in us finding out what hangs from the city's execution wall?"

Leena leaned forward, her scent—a heady mix of rose oil and smoke—washing over him. "Because we're good, Rothar. The best. You handle the blades; I handle the magic. This city's never been safe, but it's ours to dance through, and we've done it before."

There was truth in that, an unspoken bond forged in countless tight scrapes and knife's-edge escapes. Rothar let out a sigh, low and resigned. "I've always hated your luck."

"And I've always relied on yours," she replied, that teasing glimmer returning to her eyes.

Rothar pocketed the parchment and stood, casting a glance around the room to see if anyone had taken too much interest in their conversation. The room, with its grinding noise and dangerous players, seemed to hum with the promise of violence or fortune, or both. He caught the flicker of a glance from a hooded figure hunched near the hearth, and for a moment, their eyes met—gray and sharp as a dagger's blade. The figure shifted, retreating deeper into shadow. Rothar made a mental note. In Hollow-Gate, every pair of eyes could be the start of trouble.

"Then let's move before your spell runs dry," he muttered the old saying, stepping away from the table. The creak of his armor and the cold bite of steel against his thigh reminded him of the path ahead.

Leena fell into step beside him, her cloak swirling around her like a whispering phantom, the charms at her wrist chiming softly as they passed through the sea of eyes and into the smog-choked street beyond. The door of the Iron Stag banged shut behind them, cutting off the raucous din and leaving only the sound of distant hammering and the soft hiss of the wind through the narrow alleys.

The street outside was a narrow cut of stone slick with rain, pooling into iridescent puddles that reflected the faint glow of the city's oil lamps. Fog wreathed the buildings, cloaking the twisted spires and crooked chimneys that reached toward the moonless sky. HollowGate was alive at night, but not in the way most cities were. Here, it pulsed with a darker rhythm, an undercurrent of whispered deals and the scrape of blades unsheathed in silence.

Rothar's eyes swept the street, instinctively seeking hidden threats. A shadow detached itself from the mouth of an alley, just a beggar shifting in his sleep, muttering to some unseen nightmare. Rothar's shoulders relaxed a fraction. Even the damned here were restless.

Leena's voice broke the quiet, smooth as silk. "Nervous?"

"Always," Rothar replied, his tone clipped. "Only fools aren't in this city."

Her eyes gleamed under the dim lamplight, mischief sparking in their depths. "Good. Keeps things interesting."

They moved through the night, their steps synchronized out of habit. Rothar felt the weight of the job settle over him, a familiar and unwelcome shroud. They passed through Market Row, where stalls that had bustled with trade hours earlier now stood deserted, their wares hidden behind wooden shutters painted in flaking red and gold. A cat yowled from a nearby roof, its eyes catching the light like twin emeralds before it vanished into the dark.

"Tell me something," Rothar said, breaking the silence. "Why this job? You've turned down others for less risk."

Leena's stride didn't falter, but there was a momentary pause in her expression, a shadow of something that passed too quickly to name. "The Eclipse isn't just power, Rothar. The Grand Mayor is the thread holding half the city together. You pull it, and the whole weave changes."

He grunted, disapproving. "Sounds like a good way to get cut by the frayed ends."

"That's why you're here," she said, flashing him that familiar grin—reckless, beautiful, dangerous.

They turned down a narrow lane where the fog thickened, muffling sound and muting the world to a gray, formless maze. The buildings here were older, their stone facades scarred by age and neglect. Windows were shuttered tight, some nailed closed as if to ward off whatever prowled the dark. A low hum of tension crawled over Rothar's skin, each step pressing him deeper into the marrow of HollowGate's unrest.

A sound broke through the muffled silence—a creak, high and wavering, like an iron gate easing open. Rothar's hand went instinctively to the hilt of his sword, muscles coiled. He shot a glance at Leena, who had already stilled, eyes darting toward the sound.

From the dark, a figure emerged, cloaked and slender, the outline barely distinguishable from the surrounding fog. Rothar's pulse quickened, his stance shifting imperceptibly. The figure paused, then stepped forward into the dim light. It was a girl, perhaps no older than fifteen, with hollow cheeks and eyes too large for her thin face.

"Help," she rasped, voice weak, as if speaking pained her. She reached out a trembling hand, and Rothar caught the shimmer of something wet glistening between her fingers—blood. It was Kaelira.

Leena moved before Rothar could react, her boots splashing through the rain-slick street as she closed the distance. "Kaelira—what happened?" she demanded, voice sharp but not unkind.

The girl's gaze flicked between them, terror and recognition battling for control. "They didn't take her ... Lady Velora. They're watching ... even now ..."

What did she mean, they didn't—

Her voice faded into a gasp, and she crumpled, knees hitting the stone with a crack that made Rothar wince. He rushed forward, helping Leena catching her before she collapsed fully to the ground. Her skin was cold, clammy, and beneath the filth of the street, he could see bruises that told stories he didn't want to hear.

"Damn it," he muttered. "Leena, get—"

But before he could finish, a movement in the fog caught his eye. A low whistle cut through the night, sharp and clear. Rothar's heart slammed against his ribs as dark shapes emerged from the shadows, hooded figures with blades drawn, their eyes glinting in the sparse light.

"Move!" he barked, shoving the girl into Leena's arms as he drew his sword. The steel sang as it cleared the scabbard, a sound that felt like a war cry against the silence. The first attacker lunged, and Rothar sidestepped, pivoting as his blade slashed through fabric and flesh, a hot line of blood spraying against the cold stone.

Leena's voice rose behind him, chanting in the ancient, clipped syllables of her spells. Blue light crackled from her outstretched hand, arcing like lightning to strike an assailant full in the chest. The figure jerked, eyes rolling back as he collapsed in a smoldering heap.

The air filled with the metallic tang of blood and the electric bite of sorcery. Rothar's sword found another mark, the blade sinking into the soft give of muscle before he wrenched it free. A cry pierced the fog, raw and guttural, and another body fell, darkening the puddles with red.

Leena stood over the fallen girl, a protective barrier shimmering faintly around them as two more attackers advanced, their movements swift and purposeful. She met their charge with a flick of her wrist, and the barrier pulsed, sending them staggering back with shocked curses.

"Rothar!" she shouted, urgency cutting through the din.

He spun, muscles burning with the exertion, to see a blade descending toward her exposed back. Time contracted to a heartbeat; he lunged, sword intercepting with a jarring clash that rattled his bones. The assailant's eyes widened in surprise, and Rothar drove his elbow into the man's gut, following with a brutal slash that ended him.

The silence that followed was abrupt, broken only by the ragged breaths of the living. Rothar's chest heaved, the sweat and blood mingling under his armor, sticking to his skin like a second layer. The girl moaned softly, eyes fluttering as Leena laid her gently on the ground.

"Velora," she whispered, lips barely moving. "They seek the Whispering One . . ."

Then she stilled, the tension fading from her slight frame.

Leena's expression hardened, eyes narrowing as she looked up at Rothar. "She's dead," she gasped, her anger almost palpable rolling off of her. "This job just became something else."

Rothar nodded, the weight of the unspoken tightening in the air between them. They were no longer just hunting a missing noblewoman; they were stepping into a labyrinth of shadow and sorcery, where each turn promised death or something worse.

He wiped his blade clean, the steel gleaming cold under the thin glow of the city's lamps. The fog whispered around them, like the city itself murmuring secrets too dark for day.

"Then we'd better be ready," he said, the night swallowing his words as they turned back into the maze of HollowGate.

CHAPTER 2: INTO THE WORLD OF NOBLES

The Tower—the fortifications that served as the city's center of government, and the Silver Eclipse's keep—rose before them like a fortress, dark and imposing. High stone walls surrounded the compound, iron spikes glistening wickedly at the top of the gates. Rothar stood just outside, his eyes shifting over the guards stationed at the entrance.

The guards were disciplined, well-armed, and their gazes were as sharp as the blades at their sides. Tension coiled tighter in his chest, each breath amplifying the sense of walking into a den of wolves. He breathed deep to calm himself and fingered his pommel, as he was wont to do when contemplating his future.

That contemplation often came with Leena's missions.

"They don't look too friendly," Leena remarked, her voice light as she adjusted one of the charms on her wrist, its polished surface catching the last sliver of twilight.

Rothar shot her a sidelong glance, his expression set. "Don't make any trouble."

"Me? Trouble?" She flashed a grin that only deepened his wariness. "Never."

But Rothar knew better. Trouble followed Leena like the night followed the day, and her affinity for magic only stoked the flames. In a city like HollowGate, where rumors carried on the wind and envy bred violence, wielding power was an invitation for disaster. He had seen it too many times—an innocent spark igniting an inferno.

The guard at the gate, a hulking man with a scar bisecting one eyebrow, watched them approach. His eyes held the wariness of someone who knew danger when it walked through the door.

"State your business," the guard barked, his voice as rough as gravel.

Leena stepped forward, her smile disarming, an act as seamless as slipping a dagger into a sheath. "We're here on behalf of Lord Tallas," Leena said, using the name she'd been given. Tallas was a Seneschal serving The Grand Mayor, Lady Elira Voss. Without question, he was the second most powerful person in HollowGate. "He's expecting us."

The guard exchanged a quick glance with his companion, a silent conversation marked by a flicker of suspicion. Rothar's fingers twitched near his belt, a reflex he hadn't outgrown. After what seemed an eternity, the guard nodded stiffly. "Follow me."

They were led through iron gates that groaned in protest, into the estate's expansive courtyard. The stone paths were meticulously swept, framed by hedges trimmed to perfection. But it was not the manicured beauty that tightened Rothar's gut; it was the quiet. It was too still, even for a noble's estate. As they passed under a high arch carved with serpentine patterns, the air grew colder, the shadows more profound.

Rothar's eyes swept the grounds, noting the guards that shifted uneasily on their patrols and the distant silhouettes of figures cloaked in finery who turned away as they approached. There was power here, but it wasn't just wealth. It was the kind of power that whispered of blood sacrifices and deals inked in secrecy.

"I don't like this place," Rothar muttered under his breath, his voice low but firm.

Leena's lips curved in a mischievous smile. "You don't like any place that isn't a tavern."

"Too many shadows," he replied, scanning the balustrades where lanterns flickered, casting long, shivering silhouettes. "Too many secrets."

"That's why we're here, remember?" she teased, but her eyes held an edge. The flippancy was an act; he knew that as well as he knew his own scars.

They were ushered into a grand hall where the stone walls glistened with tapestries depicting battles Rothar recognized from childhood stories—conquests soaked in both valor and treachery. The air smelled faintly of incense, sweet and metallic, setting his teeth on edge. Their escort led them to a study, pushing the doors open with a creak that made the hair on Rothar's arms stand on end.

Lord Tallas awaited them, standing tall behind a mahogany desk, his dark eyes taking their measure in an instant. He was every inch the noble—clad in a deep blue tunic embroidered with silver, his fingers adorned with rings that gleamed coldly. Rothar's gaze swept over him, noting the subtle twitch in his jaw and the way his eyes lingered on Leena's wand for just a moment too long.

"Sit," Tallas commanded.

Leena obeyed smoothly, sliding into the chair with a confidence that bordered on defiance. Rothar remained stiff, perched on the edge of his seat, every sense attuned to the undercurrents of the room.

"You called us here about the disappearance," Leena began, cutting straight to the point. "But now we hear that . . ." Her voice was steady, but there was an unmistakable edge of anger behind her calm demeanor. Rothar reached out and squeezed her arm, warning. Tallas was not a man to be trifled with.

She breathed deep, calmed herself and said, "We'll need access to Lady Velora's chambers and her personal belongings. Anything she was involved in before she went missing."

Tallas's jaw clenched, a muscle jumping beneath the surface. "You'll have access to what you need. But discretion is paramount. The last thing we need is rumors."

Rothar leaned forward, his expression hard. "Why not use the city guard? This feels like their kind of problem."

The room's temperature seemed to drop as Tallas' eyes narrowed, and for the briefest moment, the carefully constructed mask slipped to reveal frustration. "The city guard has its uses," he said, his voice like a blade. "This is not one of them. Lady Velora was . . . involved in sensitive research. We need outsiders."

Rothar's pulse quickened. Research could mean anything in HollowGate, but when nobles like the Eclipse spoke of it, it often meant magic. The kind that bent laws and broke minds. He exchanged a glance with Leena, who betrayed nothing but a small, knowing smirk.

"We'll be discreet," she assured, her tone as smooth as silk. "No one will know we were here. But we need a picture, a likeness of her. Or how will we—"

He cut her off with a wave of his hand. "Of course, I predicted as much."

Tallas handed over the polished crystal orb, its faint glow casting subtle patterns of light across the room. Leena's eyes widened slightly as she took it, her fingers brushing the cool surface. The orb pulsed, and the image of Velora shimmered to life inside, suspended as though captured in a moment of living memory.

Velora's features were captivating—raven-black hair cascading in glossy waves, pale skin almost luminous, and piercing green eyes that seemed to challenge anyone who met them. The elegant embroidery of her emerald-green coat glinted faintly, a mark of her noble ties, while the crescent moon pendant at her throat shimmered with an arcane light. The faintest trace of a smirk played on her lips, as though daring the world to try and unravel her secrets.

Leena stared, entranced by the image. "She's . . . beautiful," she murmured, her voice almost too soft to carry.

Rothar, standing slightly behind her, shifted uncomfortably. The faint hum of magic emanating from the orb set his teeth on edge, but he couldn't entirely tear his gaze away. There was something about Velora's face—a mixture of strength and mystery—that held him for a moment too long. He cleared his throat, forcing himself to look away, as though snapping free from a spell.

"That thing gives me the creeps," he muttered, his tone gruff but tinged with a reluctant admiration. "Let's not forget who she's tied to, Leena.

No one wears that much elegance without hiding something dangerous underneath."

Before Leena could reply, Tallas' sharp voice cut through the moment. "Enough gawking. You have a job to do."

Tallas reached out, plucking the orb from Leena's hands with the briskness of someone who didn't tolerate wasted time. His cold gaze flicked between the two of them, lingering just long enough to press the weight of expectation into the air.

"Find her. Handle this quietly. Your reward will be waiting if you're successful," Tallas said, his voice like the snap of a whip. He gestured toward the door. "Now be gone and get to work."

Leena nodded, tucking her hair behind her ear as she adjusted the strap of her satchel. Rothar gave a curt nod, his hand instinctively brushing the hilt of his sword as they turned toward the door. The tension in the room seemed to lift slightly as they moved to leave, but the weight of the mission pressed down on their shoulders like a physical force.

Rothar glanced at Leena. "Let's hope that 're-ward' is worth whatever we're walking into."

Tallas' eyes bored into them each in turn, as if weighing the value of her word. After a moment, he nodded curtly. "Remember, discreet . . . and . . . a bit of advice . . ."

Rothar tensed as Leena stopped and turned. "Yes?"

"Don't trust anyone. Even the Eclipse."

The tension followed them as they left the study, Tallas' gaze a cold spear in their backs until the door shut with a solid thud. Rothar's jaw clenched as they made their way through the halls, the silence pressing in like a held breath.

"This has magic written all over it," Rothar muttered once they were back in the estate courtyard, the stone underfoot seeming colder now. "You heard him."

Leena rolled her eyes, the movement exaggerated as she adjusted the clasp of her cloak. "You're jumping to conclusions."

"Am I?" Rothar's voice was hard, sharp enough to cut. "You know what kind of trouble magic brings. The Eclipse wouldn't be turning to outsiders unless this was something they couldn't handle themselves."

She shrugged, her expression a perfect mask of nonchalance. "Even if magic's involved, we can handle it."

"You can handle it. I don't trust it," Rothar said, crossing his arms over his broad chest, muscles tensed like a drawn bowstring. His eyes fixed on the distant towers of the estate as if to push the thought of magic from his mind. "Magic always makes things worse."

Leena let out a sigh, a touch of frustration coloring the sound. "You act like magic's a death sentence. It's not all bad, Rothar. You've seen me use it dozens of times. It's gotten us out of more than a few tight spots."

"Just as often, it's gotten us into those tight spots," he shot back, the edge in his voice honed by memory. "The Seeker in the Broken Circle. The Guild sorcerer who nearly burned us alive. You think I forgot those? Every time magic is involved, we end up knee-deep in corpses or worse."

Leena stopped, turning to face him fully, the light from a nearby brazier casting an orange glow across her sharp features. "I control it. It doesn't control me."

Rothar's jaw flexed, the tension evident in the lines of his face. He wanted to believe her, but in a city like HollowGate, stories of sorcerers who thought the same often ended with those very sorcerers screaming into the void, consumed by powers they couldn't cage. "Until it slips out of your control and we both get burned."

For a moment, Leena's confidence faltered, replaced by something softer, more vulnerable. "I know you don't like it, Rothar. But it's part of me. I've always had to use it to survive. It's who I am."

He exhaled, the breath shuddering as he forced himself to calm down. "Fine. But if I see any signs that it's slipping out of control, we're walking away. I'm not dying for this job."

A small, rueful smile touched her lips. "Deal. Now, let's see what we can dig up."

Leena split off to gather information from the estate's staff, and Rothar kept to the periphery, skirting the stone walls and blending into the shadows. He listened, ears straining for snippets of conversation that might reveal more than intended. It wasn't long before he caught the hushed tones of two guards near the entrance to a heavily fortified wing of the estate.

"West wing's off-limits again," one muttered, casting a wary glance over his shoulder.

"Yeah, I noticed. Extra patrols, too. Must be something serious going on," the other replied, his hand tightening on the hilt of his sword.

"Just keep your mouth shut. You know how they deal with people who ask too many questions."

Rothar's brow furrowed. The west wing. Velora's chambers were in the east, which made this revelation all the more troubling. Whatever they were guarding, it wasn't part of the official story. He filed the information away, knowing they'd need to pry open that door later.

Leena's charm worked differently, allowing her to move through the estate with ease, her presence both disarming and alluring, drawing the attention of the staff and the lower nobles. She found a young maid, pale and fidgeting, whose eyes darted nervously around as if expecting someone to reprimand her.

"Lady Velora," the maid whispered when Leena coaxed her gently, "she wasn't like the others. She spent her time in the old study, always locked away with strange people. Cloaked figures came at night."

A chill swept down Leena's spine. "Do you know what she was working on?"

The maid shook her head, eyes wide. "I only know that the room felt different after. Like . . . it was alive."

Leena's fingers tightened on her cloak, masking the tremor in her hand. Magic. Strong, old magic, no doubt. She thanked the maid, and retrieved Rothar, who mumbled and cursed as they hurried, now more stealthily, to the study.

Finding it locked, Leena whispered a quick incantation and the latch clicked, opening the way. A rush of energy transferred from her body to the lock itself and she breathed deeply to still herself.

The moment she stepped inside, a charge prickled at her skin, raising the hair on her arms.

The room was in disarray, papers scattered across the desk and floor, tomes half-opened, their arcane symbols winking in the dim light. Leena's fingers trailed over the disarray on Velora's desk, her eyes narrowing as she took in the strange collection of symbols and half-scribbled notes scattered across the parchment. Among the tangled sketches of arcane diagrams and hastily scrawled spells, one image caught her eye—a crude drawing on the edge of a torn sheet, ink smudged as though Velora had tried to scratch it out.

It was an eye, simple yet unsettling, with a jagged line circling it in a thorny, twisting ring.

Leena frowned, tracing the rough outline with her finger. "This symbol . . ." she muttered, a slight shiver running down her spine. "It feels . . . familiar. Wrong, somehow."

Rothar leaned over her shoulder, studying the image with a skeptical glance. "Just another symbol?"

She shook her head, her expression unreadable. "Not this one. Symbols are intentional, especially in the kinds of circles Velora was dabbling in. This one . . . feels like a warning." She hesitated, looking up at Rothar, a flicker of unease in her eyes.

Rothar could only shrug. Time was wasting, and her pontificating was making him nervous. He wanted to rush her along, but the thoughtful look on her face told him now was not the time.

But it was another symbol, etched into the stone floor that drew her gaze finally away. It glowed faintly, a magic circle, written in some ancient, twisting script, pulsing as if breathing. She crouched, studying it. The air tasted metallic, buzzing with energy that whispered promises and warnings.

"Velora, what were you doing?" Leena murmured, fingers hovering just above the mark.

The sound of heavy boots approaching yanked her back to the present. She spun, heart pounding as Captain Varis appeared in the doorway, his expression hard as the steel he carried.

Varis was well known in HollowGate—the Captain of the Tower Guard, he was brutal and unyielding. And he looked the part. He was tall, imposing, with a gaze that cut through pretense.

His gauntleted hand rested on his well worn belt, inches from the sword he carried comfortably at his waist.

Tallas' admonition to not trust anyone, suddenly front and center in his mind, Rothar moved to stand between Leena and the new threat.

"What are you doing here?" His voice was low, dangerous.

Leena's heart thudded, but she forced a smile. "Following leads. Trying to find the Lady Velora."

His eyes narrowed, suspicion darkening them. "From what I understand, you've been given instructions. Stay out of certain areas of the estate."

The room seemed to shrink around her, the charged air pressing in. "We're just doing what we were hired to do, Captain. If Velora's trail leads here, we'll follow it."

Varis' eyes bored into hers, weighing her defiance. He stepped closer, the air between them crackling. "Be careful, sorceress. There are things in this house better left undisturbed."

As he turned away, Leena's smile faltered, unease coiling tight in her gut. Whatever secrets lay buried here, they were powerful enough to make even a man like Varis fearful.

When they returned to the courtyard again, Rothar took a moment to look at her and knew they had found trouble—as if the nasty captain was not evidence enough.

"What did you find?" he asked, his voice clipped.

"Magic," she replied, showing him the symbol she'd hastily copied. "Dark. Old. Powerful. Velora wasn't just dabbling. She was neck-deep. Did you not feel it, you big lump?" She held the paper-borne symbol before him, shielding it with her cloak from any would-be passers by.

Rothar's frown deepened into a scowl. He didn't feel the magic like Leena, but he was no less perceptive. He knew instinctively. "I told you. We need to get out of this while we can."

Leena's eyes met his, steady and determined. "We're in too deep now. Whatever she started, it's big, Rothar. We need to see this through."

He stared at the symbol, then at her, before reaching out and rolling her hands around the cursed paper as if to hide it from his own eyes—from his own rising heart rate. "Fine. But if it starts to go sideways—"

"We'll handle it," Leena interrupted, a spark of defiance in her voice. "We always do."

Rothar didn't smile. The weight of what lay ahead pressed down like a stone. He could almost feel the eyes watching from the estate windows, and it wasn't just the guards.

As they stepped back into the fog-drenched streets of HollowGate, the silence felt heavy, almost predatory. Rothar's hand drifted to the hilt of his sword, the familiar touch grounding him. They were walking a razor's edge, and he knew it wouldn't be long before it cut.

CHAPTER 3: A HIDDEN TRAIL

The fog was thicker now, creeping through the alleys like claws searching for prey. Rothar hated HollowGate at night. The city felt alive in the dark, breathing through the cracks in its cobblestone streets and hiding secrets behind every corner. It was a place where shadows whispered and the air crackled with untold stories. He stood with Leena near the entrance to the Tower, cloaked in darkness, watching the patrols move in their rigid, mechanical patterns. Each guard's step was a metronome counting down to the moment they'd make their move.

"You sure about this?" Rothar's voice was low but firm, carrying a note of warning. The cold, damp air made it feel heavier.

Leena shot him that reckless smile, a glint in her blue eyes that spoke of confidence and the thrill of the unknown. "You're always asking that. We've come this far, haven't we?"

"Yeah, and the farther we go, the worse it gets," he replied, glancing at the estate's towering walls. The sharp iron spikes crowning the stone seemed to reach for the sky, cutting into the blackness. "Magic's involved, Leena. We don't need to keep pushing this. We've got enough to walk away."

Her smile faltered for the briefest moment, replaced by a spark of irritation. "You're not seriously suggesting we back out now, are you? We're just getting to the good part."

"The good part?" Rothar's voice lowered into a growl. "You mean the part where we get killed for poking around where we don't belong?"

"Relax." She patted him on the arm, the touch lighter than a whisper. "I've got this. We're going to find out what happened to Velora, and we're going to get paid a fortune. You'll see."

Rothar shook his head, biting back the retort that hovered on the edge of his tongue. Magic. That was always the problem. He could face danger head-on with a blade in his hand, but magic was different. Unpredictable. It twisted the world, turned certainties into chaos. He had seen it twist and consume those who thought they controlled it—seen them turned from proud figures into husks, their eyes wide with the final realization that power had taken everything.

He glanced at Leena, who was already moving toward the estate, her fingers gripping her wand. She's too comfortable with it, he thought. Too confident. His instincts screamed at him that this was a mistake, but he followed anyway, unable to shake the weight in his gut.

The Tower loomed before them again, its stone walls dark and ancient, standing as a fortress in the night. But this time, they came uninvited. Rothar moved silently beside Leena, his eyes sweeping the grounds with the precision of a predator, noting every shadow, every movement.

The guards patrolled in their predictable, disciplined loops, their boots striking stone with a steady thump.

Leena paused, watching a pair of guards as they crossed the courtyard, their breath visible in the chill air. She turned to Rothar, a smile playing at her lips. "Time to make ourselves invisible."

Before he could protest, she raised her hand and murmured the words of an incantation. A shiver passed over him, bending the light and distorting their shapes. The magic wrapped around them like a second skin, chilling him with its touch. Rothar's muscles tensed as he felt the shimmer envelop him, unnatural and unsettling. This is how it always starts, he thought.

"I told you, no magic," Rothar hissed under his breath, but Leena didn't look back. She led the way, her confidence unwavering, while Rothar followed with a hand close to the hilt of his sword. The weapon's familiar weight was a reminder that he had something tangible, something real, in this maze of sorcery.

They slipped past the guards, who turned and stared into the dark with furrowed brows but saw nothing. Each step brought them closer to the entrance of the west wing—a part of the imposing structure that seemed old, and decayed with age. The air was heavy with silence. Rothar's pulse thudded in his ears, each beat a reminder of the risk they were taking. They approached the door, its iron hinges caked in rust and the wood worn with age. The estate might have been alive with riches, but this part was long forgotten, or so it seemed.

Leena whispered a hex, touched her wand to the mechanism, and the lock clicked open with a soft, reluctant groan. The door creaked as Rothar pushed it, revealing a yawning darkness beyond. They stepped inside, and the air thickened, carrying the scent of old stone, dust, and something else—something metallic and sharp, like the aftermath of lightning.

"This place hasn't been used in years," Rothar muttered, scanning the ground where footprints marred the dust. "Why is it suddenly locked down?"

Leena's fingers trailed along the wall, and she tilted her head as if listening to a song only she could hear. "It's not about who's been here. It's about what's been here."

Rothar's jaw tightened. "Magic?" He hated how the word felt in his mouth, bitter and heavy.

Leena nodded, her eyes narrowing. "Old magic. Dangerous magic."

They moved deeper into the west wing, the silence pressing around them, punctuated only by the creak of the floorboards under their boots. The walls were lined with tapestries, their colors faded into ghostly shades, scenes of battles long past where armored figures clashed under storm-dark skies. The deeper they went, the more the air thrummed, vibrating with energy that even Rothar could feel.

Ahead of them, double doors loomed, their iron handles wrapped in tarnished ivy carvings. Rothar raised a hand, signaling Leena to stay back as he crouched and examined the floor. Fresh scuff marks interrupted the dust.

"Someone's been through here recently," he said, his voice barely more than a breath.

"Velora?" Leena whispered, though she sounded more hopeful than certain.

Rothar shook his head. "No. This is too deliberate. Whoever came through knew what they were doing."

He pushed open the doors, and they entered a large, circular room. An altar stood at its center, carved from obsidian and inlaid with symbols that glowed with an unnatural blue light. The room was drenched in a thick, pulsing energy that made Rothar's skin crawl. The light pulsed like a heartbeat, casting fractured, jittering shadows across the walls.

Leena's eyes widened as she approached the altar, her fascination momentarily eclipsing her caution. "This is it. This is what Velora was after."

Rothar moved, his arm shooting out to grip hers before she could step closer. "Don't. You don't know what that thing will do."

She met his eyes, irritation flashing across her face. "I'm not going to touch it, Rothar. But this—this is the key. Velora was trying to summon something."

"Summon what?" His eyes searched hers for an answer he hoped didn't exist.

"I don't know," she admitted, her voice a mix of frustration and awe. "Daemon maybe? I intend to find out."

Rothar's grip tightened, grounding them both in the moment. "Not here. We've seen enough."

Leena hesitated, torn between curiosity and the trust she knew she owed him. Finally, she nodded, but her eyes lingered on the glowing runes as they turned to leave. The air still hummed behind them, a silent promise of danger.

They had barely made it halfway back down the hall when Rothar froze, lifting a hand. Footsteps echoed from the direction of the entrance, steady and purposeful. The hair on the back of his neck rose.

"Someone's coming," he whispered, pressing Leena into the shadows beside a cracked pillar. The stone was cold against his back, and the rough surface bit into his skin, but he barely noticed. His heart thudded as the door creaked open and figures filed in, dark silhouettes framed by the dim light from the corridor.

Silver Eclipse enforcers. Their expressions were stony, eyes alert as they fanned out, the gleam of their armor muted by the fog that had seeped in. One of them stopped, head tilting as if catching a scent. Rothar's hand moved to his sword, slow and deliberate.

"They're searching for something," he mouthed, his breath visible in the chill.

Leena's eyes met his, wide with questions she couldn't voice. She raised her hand, murmuring an incantation so softly that even Rothar could barely hear it. A faint shimmer of light appeared at the end of the hall, flickering like a distant torch. The guards turned, drawn to the movement.

Rothar seized the moment, tugging Leena behind him as they moved, quick and silent, through the shadows. Each step felt like an eternity, the sound of their breaths muffled by the pulse of blood in his ears. A guard's voice rang out behind them, sharp and questioning.

"Who's there?"

They reached the far end of the hall and slipped out a side door, the cool night air striking their faces as they emerged into the courtyard. The fog swirled around them, thicker than before, a living thing that wrapped them in its embrace.

They didn't stop until they reached the relative safety of a narrow alleyway, the stones slick with moisture. Rothar leaned against the wall, catching his breath as Leena steadied herself, eyes blazing with excitement.

"We need to stop," Rothar said, the words rough and edged with exhaustion. "This isn't just a missing person anymore. We're dealing with forces we can't control."

Leena's gaze was fierce, unyielding. "No. We're close, Rothar. Velora was trying to summon something, and whatever it is, it's powerful. We need to understand what she was doing before it's too late."

"And what if we get caught in the middle of it?" He pushed off the wall, fists clenched as he tried to shake the image of the altar from his mind. "You're playing with fire, Leena."

"I'm not playing," she said sharply. She reached into her coat and pulled out a crumpled piece of parchment, thrusting it into his hands. "I found this in the west wing. It mentions something called 'The Whispering One.' If Velora was trying to summon it, we need to know why."

Rothar stared at the paper, the foreign symbols meaningless to him but chilling in their intent. The name alone made his skin crawl. "The Whispering One?"

Leena nodded, the defiance in her eyes tempered by worry. "I know someone in the city who deals in this kind of knowledge. Forbidden texts, arcane artifacts—he's deep in the black market. If anyone can help us, it's him."

"Black market?" Rothar's distrust flared, and he felt a familiar tightness in his chest. "You're really diving headfirst into this."

She took a step closer, her face inches from his. "We don't have a choice. If Velora's summoning something dangerous and the Silver Eclipse is involved, we can't just walk away. It's only a matter of time before this engulfs the whole city."

Rothar's gaze drifted to the fog, the tendrils shifting and coiling as if listening. His instincts screamed at him to cut and run. They were mercenaries, not heroes. Their job was to find Velora, not unravel a mystery that could consume them all. But he couldn't shake the feeling that turning away now would mean something worse was coming for them, no matter where they hid.

He sighed, the sound heavy with resignation. "Fine. We'll talk to your contact. But if this spirals, we're pulling out. No more shadows. No more magic."

A flicker of relief crossed Leena's face, quickly replaced by determination. "Deal. But trust me, Rothar—this will give us the answers we need."

He didn't answer, just stared into the shifting fog. They were in too deep now, entangled in something that whispered of death and power. And somewhere behind them, beyond the safety of the stone walls and twisting alleys, the dark eyes of the estate seemed to follow their every move.

They turned and disappeared into the night, the weight of their discovery pressing down like unseen hands, and the cold, watchful gaze of HollowGate's shadows trailing them with silent intent.

CHAPTER 4: INTO THE SHADOWS

The first rays of early morning light struggled to pierce through the fog that hung like a living shroud over HollowGate. The pale, silvery glow barely touched the cobblestones, where dampness clung to every crevice. Rothar moved through the city's maze-like streets with Leena at his side, their pace steady but cautious. The chill that seeped into his bones wasn't from the weather—it was the sense of unseen eyes watching them, tracking their every move as they ventured deeper into this part of the city.

This quarter of HollowGate was an enigma. Each cracked stone and warped wooden shutter seemed to whisper secrets no one dared speak aloud. The shadows here felt different, deeper and alive. Rothar walked with deliberate strides, his mind coiled with tension, muscles taut beneath his worn armor. The persistent fog rolling in from the Dark Water muffled the sound of their footsteps, and the surrounding city shifted with a subtle, unsettling energy.

"You sure this contact of yours is reliable?" Rothar's question was almost drowned out by the murmur of the waking city, but he never stopped scanning the rooftops. Black birds perched above, their beady eyes glinting like tiny omens as they followed the pair's progress. Rothar's brow furrowed as he paced, considering their options. "We don't have to see witches. We could go see Joren. He's worked with the Eclipse before; he'd have an idea of what we're up against. He's . . . resourceful." His voice carried a hint of hesitation.

Leena snorted, stopped and looked at him, her eyes narrowed. She folded her arms. "Resourceful? The man's a snake, Rothar. He trades secrets like coin and has loyalties as steady as a shadow at dusk."

"Which is exactly why he'd know what we're dealing with," Rothar replied. "If anyone has knowledge about the Silver Eclipse or . . . anything worse, it's him."

Leena shook her head, a wary look in her eyes. "Only if we have no other options. His kind of help comes with a price." She turned back to their plans, her reluctance clear. Leena glanced at him again, her expression sharp, shadows darkening the pale blue of her eyes. "The witch is reliable enough. Talira has survived in this trade longer than most. If anyone has the answers we need, it's her."

"Survival doesn't mean trust," Rothar muttered, resolved. His gaze shifted to an alley that seemed to breathe as the fog rolled through it in slow waves.

"It's the best we've got," Leena said, a touch of irritation sharpening her voice. She turned a corner, her boots scuffing against the slick cobblestones. "Unless you'd rather go in blind?"

Rothar bit back a response. They were too far in now, and arguing with Leena's resolve was as pointless as trying to hold back the sea. He followed her down a narrow stairway, the steps worn smooth from countless feet, until they emerged in the dim glow of the under market, a little-known place below the Grand Bazaar which even this was beginning to come alive the sound of shops and temporary facades being thrown up and opened. The echo of hucksters and pitchmen would soon join the muffled cacophony.

The underground market was a labyrinth of hidden exchanges and whispered deals, alive even at this hour with the low hum of voices. Some said it was part of the Bones of Hollow-Gate, the network of ancient hidden dungeons and dark passageways that laced beneath the city above. But Rother had no way of proving such and the thought made him shudder.

The light from torches cast long, jittery shadows against the stone walls, making them seem to shift and dance. Vendors hawked their wares, not with calls and whistles, but with furtive gestures and sidelong glances, faces hidden by hoods or elaborate masks. The air was thick with the mingling scents of burning herbs, metal, and the faint, acrid undertone of forbidden magic.

Rothar felt a prickle at the back of his neck as they passed a stall draped in tattered red cloth. Crystal orbs, each filled with swirling smoke that shimmered like trapped souls, seemed to follow their movement. The merchant behind the table, a wiry man with a crooked smile, caught Leena's eye and raised an eyebrow. She gave a subtle nod, an acknowledgment so slight that Rothar almost missed it.

She belonged here in a way that gnawed at him like an old wound.

"Keep your guard up," Rothar said, more to himself than to her.

Leena's lips curved in a faint smile, but she didn't look back. "Always do."

They wove through the narrow pathways of the market, stepping over the twisted roots of a tree that had pushed through the stone floor over decades. Its gnarled limbs curled upward like talons, and the thin branches overhead formed a shivering canopy. Rothar shifted his weight, instinctively placing himself between Leena and a group of cloaked figures huddled near a brazier. Their faces were hidden, but their muttered conversation was a mix of guttural growls and melodic cadences, sending an uneasy thrill down his spine.

Leena quickened her pace, leading him down a side tunnel lit only by a single oil lamp. Here, the shadows pressed in more tightly, the air growing cooler with each step. At the end of the passage sat a small stall crammed with scrolls, crystal fragments, and ancient tomes bound in cracked leather. Runes carved into the wood glowed faintly, casting shifting, ominous patterns on the walls.

Talira stood behind the cluttered stall, moving with the practiced calm of someone who had seen everything and feared little. Her long, gray hair was pulled back, accentuating the sharp angles of her face. Dark, depthless eyes settled on Leena first, then shifted to Rothar, assessing him in a way that made his skin crawl.

"Leena," Talira said, her voice soft but edged with a note of caution. "It's been some time."

"It has," Leena replied, her smile tight. "I wish it were under better circumstances."

Talira's eyes flicked back to Rothar, assessing, before she returned her attention to Leena. "And you brought a guardian. Wise."

Rothar's jaw tightened, but he stayed silent. He wasn't here for her games or cryptic remarks. Nor was he a simple guardian. It galled him, these wizardly types and their condescension toward those who chose steel over whispers.

Leena slid a folded piece of parchment from her coat and placed it on the counter. It looked oddly out of place among the ancient, more sinister items cluttering Talira's space. "We found this at the Tower. Velora was working on something—summoning something."

Talira's fingers, long and thin like the talons of a crow, unfolded the parchment with deliberate care. The moment her eyes scanned the symbols, a shadow passed over her face, darkening her features. "The Whispering One," she whispered, the name sliding from her lips like a curse. Rothar felt a chill run down his spine, the market's distant noise seeming to recede until all he heard was the thud of his heartbeat.

"What do you know about it?" Rothar's question came out rough, more a demand than a request.

Talira's gaze met his, glimmering with a mix of pity and warning. "More than you'd care to know, I suspect. The Whispering One is older than recorded time, from before the Ishkalians who betrayed nature, and even before the Qorlan Dynasty, the collapsed civilizations from eons past whose pursuit of forbidden lore cast our world to black. It is beyond any magic you've faced. It feeds on secrets, on knowledge best left untouched, drawn to power like a moth to flame. Summoning it isn't just dangerous; it's catastrophic. Velora is toying with a force that she can't contain."

Leena leaned in, eyes bright and relentless. "Can it be stopped? Controlled?"

A shadow of a smile touched Talira's lips, a sad curve that spoke of buried memories. "Those who've tried have not lived to share their stories."

Rothar's patience frayed, snapping like a taut wire. "Then why pursue this? If it's beyond control, what's the point of knowing more?" His voice was taut with anger, but beneath it, a deep-rooted fear throbbed.

Leena's gaze locked onto his, fierce and unyielding. "Because if Velora is close, it could mean the end of us all—and this beautiful city we live in. If we don't understand it, we're as good as blind when it strikes again."

Rothar clenched his fists. "Beautiful city . . . Hah." The room seemed smaller, the light from the runes flickering like anxious breaths. This was how it always started: curiosity bleeding into obsession, and obsession turning into disaster. Memories surged—charred stone, screams that wouldn't stop echoing. He pushed them back down, hard.

Talira's voice cut through the tension. "If you're serious, you'll need more than scraps of parchment and guesses. The ritual scrolls Velora studies are no doubt locked in the archives of the Silver Eclipse Tower. Deep. Underneath. Getting to them will be no simple task. Even the guard does not go there. Reaching them will take more than brute force . . . or stealthy lock picks."

Leena tilted her head, suspicion flickering in her eyes. "What do you mean?"

Talira stepped around the cluttered table, her fingers trailing lightly over the jagged edges of crystal fragments and the spines of crumbling tomes. She stopped before a small, locked coffer, which opened with a subtle twist of her hand. From within, she pulled out a shard of glass-like stone, its surface swirling with faint, silvery light.

"This," Talira said, holding it up so it caught the flickering glow of the runes, "is your key."

Rothar's brow furrowed. "A shard of fancy rock? We're supposed to sneak into one of the most heavily guarded places in HollowGate with that?"

A shadow of a smirk curled Talira's lips. "Not everything can be solved with steel, mercenary. This shard is a fragment of the Tower's very foundation—enchanted long ago to interact with its wards. With the right incantation, it will open a path beneath the Tower into the catacombs. Velora would've used it to move unseen."

Leena reached for it, her fingers brushing the shard. A soft hum resonated in the air, sending a faint chill up her arm. "And the incantation?" she asked, her voice quiet, almost reverent.

Talira hesitated, her gaze narrowing. "It's a spell of old magic, tied to the Tower itself. It will weaken the warding long enough for you to slip inside. But"—her voice grew harder—"use it sparingly. It will alert the Tower's defenses if you linger too long. And once you've activated it, the way will close behind you."

Leena's fingers tightened around the shard, its glow reflecting in her determined eyes. "That's all we need."

"Is it?" Rothar's voice was sharp, his wariness unmistakable. "You're forgetting the cost." He turned to Talira, his jaw tight. "What do you want?"

Talira's smile deepened, a glimmer of triumph in her eyes. "A share of whatever relics or knowledge you uncover. The Tower's secrets are its true treasures, and I intend to claim my due."

"This isn't a game, Leena," Rothar said, his voice low, measured. "You're bargaining with more than just coin."

Leena turned to him, her expression fierce, unwavering. "Do you want to survive this, Rothar? Because we won't if we don't know what we're facing."

The room seemed to hold its breath as the two locked eyes. Rothar searched her face for any trace of doubt and found none. The weight of inevitability pressed down on him like heavy mail. His hand drifted to the hilt of his sword—a reflex when words failed him. Finally, he gave a sharp, reluctant nod.

"Deal," Leena said, voice steady. The pact was struck.

There was always a deal with Leena.

Talira extended her hand, palm up, the shard glinting faintly. "Then take it—and do not squander it. The incantation is etched into its core. It will guide you when the time comes."

Leena took the shard, holding it carefully, almost reverently. Rothar glared at it warily, muttering under his breath about magic being more trouble than it was worth.

Before they could speak further, a commotion rippled through the market. The torchlight cast jagged shadows as vendors shifted uneasily. Rothar's gaze darted to the source, catching the gleam of silver insignias on dark uniforms. The enforcers of the Silver Eclipse were here, their eyes cold and searching.

"They're here," Rothar said, his voice low and urgent. The tension coiled in his muscles, ready to spring.

Talira's face darkened. "You've drawn attention. This place is not for amateurs." She muttered an incantation, her fingers moving in quick, precise gestures. A shimmer enveloped Rothar and Leena, blurring their outlines, blending them into the restless shadows of the market.

"It won't last long," Talira whispered. "Go. Now."

Rothar grabbed Leena's arm, pulling her into motion as the enforcers pushed deeper into the market. Their shouts cut through the low hum of voices, sharp and commanding. Vendors' protests met with indifference. The dark market pulsed with collective unease, a living thing sensing danger.

A brazier toppled near them, embers scattering across the stone like a spray of angry fireflies. Rothar kicked it aside, clearing their path as they wove through the chaos. His eyes swept for exits, calculating distances, reading threats. A woman's scream tore through the place as an enforcer grabbed her, demanding answers. Rothar's breath came faster, his chest tight with the push of adrenaline.

"Move faster," he urged, his voice rough. They turned into an alley barely wide enough for them to pass, the walls slick with dew and old grime. The narrow space funneled the noise behind them, amplifying the thud of boots and the hiss of commands.

Leena shot him a look, defiance glinting in her eyes even as they ran. She thrived on moments like this, and it made something in his chest clench—fear, anger, and something more complicated.

They ducked into a dark alcove, the rough stone biting into Rothar's back as he pressed himself against it. Leena's breath came in sharp gasps beside him, her eyes searching his for a moment before flicking back to the street. The shouts of the enforcers grew distant, the noise fading like a storm moving on.

Only then did Rothar exhale, the tension draining enough for anger to flare in its wake. "This is exactly what I warned you about," he said, voice a low growl. "Magic draws attention, and now we're hunted."

Leena's eyes narrowed, her tone matching his in intensity. "This isn't just about magic, Rothar. This is about survival. If Velora's summoning wasn't stopped, then something worse is coming. We need to be ready."

Rothar stared at her, searching for some sign of doubt. Instead, he found a determination that both infuriated and fascinated him. He looked away, the alley around them pressing close, the shadows feeling more like a cage than a sanctuary.

"If this goes wrong, it's on you," he said finally, the words leaving a bitter taste.

Leena's jaw set, the corner of her mouth lifting in a smirk that didn't reach her eyes. "Then we make sure it doesn't."

They stood in silence, the market's echoes dying around them. Rothar's doubts gnawed at him, but he knew turning back now was no longer an option. The path ahead was steeped in shadow and danger, but it was the only path left.

With a last glance at the street behind them, they stepped out into the shifting fog, ready for whatever hunted them in the heart of Hollow-Gate.

CHAPTER 5: THE FORBIDDEN ARCHIVES

The safehouse felt like a cage.

Shadows crept along the cracked walls, thrown by the flickering candle that struggled against the oppressive dimness. The single flame sputtered, fighting against drafts that slithered through the room and carried the faint, acrid tang of The Sprawl, HollowGate's largest and most decrepit ward. A cracked window offered a glimpse of the outside world—a sliver of crooked, filthy streets where the Dark Water's mist still clung to the stones like an old secret, even as evening approached. Rothar leaned against the rough, splintered edge of a table strewn with daggers, maps, and vials of unknown liquids, each labeled in Leena's precise handwriting. The room hummed with tension, alive with the muted sounds of a city that never truly slept.

Distant shouts of street vendors closing their stalls from the Grand Bazaar mingled with the rustle of rats scuttling through garbage heaps in the nearby warrens. Rothar's ears caught the whisper of footsteps beyond the alley, too light and quick to be drunks or beggars. He frowned, turning his attention to Leena, who sat cross-legged on the floor. Her posture was rigid, her lips moving in a whisper as she chanted over her wand that glowed with a cold, blue light. The hum of her incantation vibrated through the wooden planks, filling the space with an electric pulse that tightened the air and made Rothar's skin prickle.

The sharp, metallic scent of her magic coiled around him like a warning. His eyes narrowed as he watched the end of the wand's eerie glow dance across her determined face. "We're about to break into the Silver Eclipse's vault of secrets, and you think a trinket will keep us alive?" His voice was low, but it carried the bite of doubt.

Leena's fingers paused for a fraction of a second before she resumed the delicate weave of her spell. Her gaze remained fixed on the focus, as if willing it to answer him instead. "It will keep us unseen long enough. You've trusted worse odds, Rothar."

He looked away, jaw clenching, as he traced the grain of the rough table with calloused fingers. Memories of other gambles, the kind that cost more than they paid, surfaced unbidden. "Worse odds didn't involve magic."

Her laugh was sharp, a sound that bounced off the splintered walls like the creak of a door left ajar. "Everything involves magic in HollowGate, whether you admit it or not. You either use it, or you end up at the mercy of those who do."

Their eyes met, and the flickering candlelight carved deep lines across their faces. Rothar saw the defiance in her eyes, the unyielding belief that what she was doing was right. The silence stretched, heavy with unspoken stories and battles they'd fought together. His fingers flexed around the hilt of a dagger, its cold steel a comfort amidst the chaos.

Without another word, he stepped forward and blew out the candle, plunging the room into darkness broken only by the cold, blue glow of Leena's wand. The hum of her magic pulsed like a heartbeat, guiding them forward.

Once again they approached the Tower. But this time, things felt different. Darker. The construction loomed like a slumbering beast under the moon's pale and unforgiving gaze. High walls stretched upward like jagged teeth, crowned with iron spikes that glistened with frost. The air was sharp and bitter, heavy with the promise of violence. Guards moved along the battlements with mechanical precision, their boots striking stone in a rhythm that reverberated into the stillness of the night. Torchlight flickered, casting their shadows into elongated specters that seemed to watch every corner of the grounds.

Rothar and Leena crouched in the shadow of a crumbling stone archway, where frost clung to the ancient masonry like a second skin. The cold bit through their clothes, but neither spoke of it. The air between them was tense, brittle as glass, as they studied the fortress that lay before them.

"This feels wrong," Rothar muttered, his voice a gravelly whisper. His hand brushed the hilt of his sword reflexively.

Leena shot him a sharp look, her blue eyes glinting in the moonlight. "It always feels wrong, doesn't it?" she said softly. She reached into her satchel and pulled out the shard Talira had given her. It pulsed faintly, the silver light within rippling like disturbed water. "But we don't have a choice."

He said nothing, watching as she turned the shard in her fingers, its glow illuminating the determination etched on her face. Without another word, she nodded toward a section of the tower's base, a stretch of wall that seemed unremarkable in every way. Rothar frowned. "That's it?" he asked.

Leena smirked faintly. "You'd be surprised how much magic prefers the mundane. Talira said it's tied to the foundation—so yes, that's it."

They moved quickly and silently, slipping through the darkness like wraiths. The guard patrols, precise as they were, offered narrow windows of opportunity, and Rothar's muscles tensed with every step as they crossed the cobbled courtyard. The frost on the ground crackled faintly beneath his boots, and he cursed under his breath.

Leena reached the wall first, her fingers tightening around the shard. She pressed it to the stone, its light flaring brighter. The wall pulsed faintly, rippling as though the stone itself were alive. The shard hummed, a low, resonant sound that seemed to vibrate through the very air. Rothar stepped closer, his hand resting uneasily on the pommel of his sword.

"Now what?" he asked, his tone guarded.

Leena didn't answer immediately. She closed her eyes, whispering the incantation that Talira had taught her. The words spilled from her lips in a cadence that was both melodic and harsh, as if the air itself resisted the ancient magic. The shard's light intensified, casting eerie shadows that danced across the frost-covered ground. Rothar felt the weight of the spell settle over them, heavy and oppressive, as though the night itself held its breath.

The wall shuddered. Cracks spiderwebbed across its surface, the mortar crumbling away to reveal a jagged, narrow passage that led downward into inky darkness. Cold, damp air spilled from the opening, carrying with it the faint scent of earth and something metallic—something old.

"Magical doors," Rothar muttered, his unease thick in his voice. "Always so inviting."

Leena shot him a sharp glance, her hand tightening on the shard as the passage yawned open before them. "It's this or the guards. Your choice."

He grunted, stepping forward reluctantly, his sword drawn. The darkness seemed to close around him as he entered, his boots scraping against uneven stone. Leena followed, the shard's faint light casting wavering shadows against the rough walls. The passage sloped steeply, the air growing colder with every step, as though the Tower itself rejected their presence.

The tunnel twisted and turned, the walls narrowing in places until Rothar's broad shoulders brushed the damp stone. The silence was suffocating, broken only by the faint drip of water that echoed somewhere in the distance. The shard's light began to dim as they descended deeper, forcing Leena to hold it closer to see the uneven ground beneath their feet.

"Leena," Rothar said quietly, his voice cutting through the stillness. "What's at the end of this?"

Leena's expression was tight, unreadable. "Something Velora thought was worth hiding."

Rothar growled low in his throat. "I hate magic."

The passage ended abruptly, opening into a cavernous chamber that stretched farther than the shard's faint glow could reach. Rothar squinted into the darkness, his hand tightening on his sword. The floor beneath their feet was smoother here, worn down by centuries of use, and the walls were carved with ancient runes that pulsed faintly as if reacting to their presence.

Leena stepped forward, holding the shard aloft. Its light flared briefly, illuminating a central dais in the chamber's heart. On it lay a large, circular stone door, its surface inscribed with intricate, overlapping symbols. Rothar's unease deepened as he stared at it, the faint hum of magic prickling against his skin.

"This isn't a vault," he said. "It's a tomb."

Leena didn't reply immediately, her focus on the door. "It doesn't matter what it is. What matters is what's inside."

The shard's glow dimmed further as Leena approached the dais, her voice low as she murmured another incantation. The runes on the door began to shift, sliding and turning like pieces of a puzzle. Rothar felt the tension in the air grow heavier, pressing against his chest like a weight.

"Whatever you're doing, do it fast," he muttered, his eyes scanning the darkness. The chamber seemed to pulse with life, the shadows moving just out of reach of the shard's glow.

Leena didn't answer, her concentration unbroken. The runes on the door aligned with a sharp,

metallic click, and the air around them vibrated with power. The door shifted, stone grinding
against stone as it began to open, revealing a
narrow stairway descending even deeper into the
earth.

Rothar exhaled slowly, the sound almost a
growl. "This better be worth it."

Leena gave him a faint, tired smile. "If it wasn't,
Velora wouldn't have risked it."

They stepped forward together, the faint light
from the shard leading them into the waiting
darkness below.

They slipped into a corridor shrouded in darkness. The air was thick, laced with the musty
scent of old parchment, oil smoke from torches long extinguished, and the faint tang of rust.
The walls seemed to lean inward, their stones
shifting subtly, as if the estate itself was watching. Rothar's instincts, honed from years of battle
and betrayal, screamed at him to draw his blade.

"Stay close," he muttered, his voice barely a
breath.

Leena's footsteps whispered behind him, a
measured rhythm interrupted only by the faint

rustle of fabric and the occasional tap of a charm brushing metal. The corridor twisted into narrower passages, each turn pressing the cold stone walls tighter against them. The floor was slick, the dampness seeping into the worn soles of their boots.

They reached a set of double doors, carved with intricate sigils that seemed to writhe as the light from Leena's wand brushed over them. Rothar's jaw clenched as he watched the runes shift, the metallic tang in the air stinging the back of his throat. Leena's fingers hovered just above the carvings, tracing the shapes without touching.

"Wards," she whispered, the word tight with tension. Her eyes fluttered closed as she chanted, her breath quickening, matching the heartbeat of the sigils themselves. Rothar stood watch, every muscle coiled and ready, ears straining for the sound of approaching footsteps or the clang of armor. The surrounding room seemed to hold its breath.

The glow from the sigils flickered and dimmed, the oppressive weight in the air lifting. Leena's shoulders sagged, a bead of sweat tracing a path down her temple. She opened her eyes, the blue light in them dimmed with exhaustion.

"Done," she said, her voice strained but resolute.

The doors groaned as they opened, revealing the archives beyond. Rows of towering shelves stretched toward a vaulted ceiling where thin, slitted windows let in pale beams of moonlight. The cold light cast silken threads across the room, illuminating dust motes that danced in the air. Each shelf groaned under the weight of books bound in cracked leather and scrolls marked with arcane symbols. The air here was colder, alive with an unseen pulse, as if the knowledge within was restless, waiting to be disturbed.

Leena moved to a central table, her fingers brushing aside brittle parchment and brittle quills with the reverence of someone searching for a lost truth. The sound of paper rustling and the scrape of wood echoed, sharp against the silence. Among the pages were diagrams of sigils, fragmented incantations, and letters written in a neat, formal script. She paused, lifting one of the pages closer to the light.

"Rothar," she said, her voice tight. "Look at this."

He stepped closer, glancing at the page she held up. It was a letter bearing the wax seal of the Silver Eclipse—unmistakable, even in the flickering torchlight.

"Velora's funding," Leena murmured, her voice a mix of awe and disbelief. "They were bankrolling her research. 'Binding rituals for celestial entities'—this was sanctioned."

Rothar's jaw tightened as he scanned the letter. "And then they tried to bury her," he muttered darkly. "Typical. She probably realized they'd never let her keep what she found."

"Or she realized they couldn't control it," Leena added, her expression darkening as her fingers brushed the fragmented notes. "They didn't care about the danger of whatever it was—just the power."

Rothar's voice was grim. "And when they realized it would destroy them too, they sent us to clean up their mess."

Leena's lips pressed into a thin line, her eyes narrowing. "We should've charged more."

"No doubt," he said. "Understatement."

Leena was quiet. Her hands trembled as she sifted further through the scattered documents on the altar, her eyes scanning the frenzied scrawl of Velora's notes.

"Find anything else?" Rothar's voice was low, each word dropping into the quiet like a stone into deep water.

"Yes." Her fingers found a scroll marked with dark, hurried script. The ink had bled into the edges, as if written in a frenzy. "It's Velora's. This answers everything. She was crafting a binding ritual, trying to tether the essence of the Whispering One, I presume."

Rothar's chest tightened as he moved to read over her shoulder, eyes skimming the alien symbols and erratic handwriting. "Binding it? That's not ambition—it's insanity."

Leena's hand shook as she read, the chill in the room seeping deeper into her bones as the implications settled over them like frost. "She didn't just want power. She wanted control,

Rothar. Enough to challenge anyone who dared to stand against her."

The words twisted in Rothar's mind, pulling memories from dark places. He had seen this before—seen what happened when power seduced someone past the point of reason. Before he could voice his thoughts, a sound cut through the silence: the sharp, metallic clink of armor. His eyes snapped to the far side of the room, where shadows shifted, and dark forms emerged. Enforcers, their insignias gleaming like silver threats, stepped into the light.

"Well, isn't this an unfortunate surprise?" Captain Varis' voice was smooth, cold as the steel at his side. He moved with the assurance of someone who expected victory, his eyes hard as they settled on Leena and Rothar. "Hand over what you've found, and maybe we'll let you walk out with your lives."

Rothar's hand found the hilt of his sword, the leather creaking under his grip. "I'm not one for negotiation."

The enforcers shifted, the tension in the room coiling like a spring about to snap. Leena's eyes darted between them, her fingers tightening around her wand.

"Don't," Rothar said, his voice sharp and edged with warning. But it was too late. The room exploded into motion, the clash of steel shattering the silence. Rothar met the first enforcer head-on, parrying the downward strike with a grunt as sparks burst between their blades. The scent of sweat and blood mingled with the musty air as he spun, elbowing the guard in the jaw and sending him sprawling.

Leena's voice rose in a chant, the syllables rapid and strained. A wave of energy rippled out, knocking an enforcer off his feet with a flash of blue light. The air hissed with the sharp tang of magic, filling Rothar's nostrils and making his pulse quicken. Varis lunged, his sword slicing the air with a deadly hum. Rothar blocked, muscles straining as the force of the blow drove him back a step. The captain's grin was a thin, cruel slash as he pressed forward, eyes gleaming with the thrill of the fight.

"You're outmatched," Varis snarled, pushing Rothar to the brink.

Rothar twisted, pivoting on his heel and slamming his shoulder into Varis' chest. The captain staggered, surprise flaring in his eyes before rage overtook it. The shout of another enforcer rang out behind them, drawing Rothar's attention for a heartbeat too long. Pain lanced through his arm as Varis' blade nicked his flesh, just where the mail ended, hot and wet beneath the torn fabric of his gambeson sleeve.

The taste of blood filled Rothar's mouth as he clenched his jaw against the pain. Leena's voice rose, a frantic chant as the glow around her flared and sputtered. The spell wavered, the energy spiraling out of control. A bolt of raw magic arced across the room, striking a lantern and sending flames racing up a nearby shelf. The fire roared to life, the dry parchment crackling as the heat surged.

"Leena!" Rothar's shout cut through the chaos as smoke coiled into the air, thick and acrid, searing his lungs.

Her eyes met his, wide with panic before focus returned to her features. "We have to move. Now."

He blocked another strike, deflecting the enforcer's blade with a screech that rang in his ears. Without another word, he grabbed Leena's arm and yanked her toward a side passage that loomed like a dark wound in the stone. They stumbled into the narrow corridor, flames roaring behind them, licking at their backs like a living thing.

The passage narrowed, the cold, damp walls closing in. Condensation dripped in steady beats, echoing their ragged breaths as they descended. The sounds of pursuit faded behind them, replaced by the rush of their footsteps and the rhythmic pounding of their hearts. Were they entering the Bones of the city? Were they fleeing to something worse than Varis and his minions?

They burst into a tunnel that reeked of stagnant water and decay, the stench slamming into them like a physical blow. Rothar leaned against the stone, chest heaving, the gash on his arm stinging with each pulse. He glanced at Leena, who was slumped against the opposite wall, blood trailing down her brow and smearing her cheek.

"You need to rest," he said, voice rough with exhaustion and concern he hadn't meant to reveal. "This obsession is going to get us both killed."

Leena wiped at the blood, eyes fierce even as exhaustion shadowed her features. "No, it's going to save us. You must trust me, Rothar. We don't have a choice."

His eyes narrowed as he searched her face for any sign of doubt, finding only determination etched deep. The silence wrapped around them, heavy and suffocating. The Bones of HollowGate seemed to mock him in hissing whispers, reminding him that the choice to turn back had passed long ago.

With a reluctant nod, Rothar pushed off the wall, his movements tight with pain and tension. "Then let's make sure we survive long enough to regret it."

Together, they moved deeper into the maze of tunnels, their footsteps swallowed by the darkness. Behind them, the echoes of flames and battle lingered like a distant promise that their path was set—and there was no going back.

The air grew thicker, a stale, suffocating presence that clung to their skin. Each turn revealed another stretch of endless shadow, the low, steady drip of water the only sound breaking the oppressive silence. Rothar's grip tightened around his sword, his gaze shifting warily to each dark corner, the weight of the Bones pressing down on him like a stone.

"Are you sure you know the way out?" he muttered, his voice echoing back at him in the close air.

Leena's response was barely a whisper. "I know what I can sense—the wards, the faint energy flows. They're all leading upward." Her wand glowed faintly, casting a dim blue light that stretched feebly against the shadows. "But the magic here . . . it's old. It could be twisted."

Rothar's jaw tightened, the muscles straining with the effort to stay calm. They pressed on, step by careful step, their every movement deliberate, wary of traps and hidden dangers. Shadows seemed to reach out as they passed, their elongated forms twisting on the walls like mocking phantoms, and Rothar's instincts screamed at him that they weren't alone.

A sudden sound—a faint scrape, like nails dragging against stone—caught his attention. He halted, motioning for Leena to stop. She glanced at him, her eyes wide, and listened, her body tense.

"It's following us," he whispered, a barely perceptible tremor in his voice.

They both turned, their gazes piercing the dark corridor behind them, but nothing moved. Still, the air felt charged, as if something unseen and ancient lingered, watching.

Rothar gestured forward. "We need to move—now."

They quickened their pace, their footsteps nearly silent but hurried. The darkness pressed in closer, the stale air thickening with every step. Leena's charm flickered, and she gritted her teeth, muttering under her breath as she tried to hold the magic steady. Rothar glanced back, certain he saw movement in the darkness, a slithering, unnatural shape keeping pace with them.

A sudden rush of cold swept through the tunnel, and Leena stumbled, catching herself against the wall. The shadows seemed to thicken, coiling like mist around their ankles, pulling them back. Rothar seized her arm, pulling her forward with a fierce urgency.

"Keep going! Whatever this is, we're not stopping here," he growled.

Leena pushed forward, her breathing shallow as they wound through the narrow passage, her magic light casting strange, shifting shadows along the walls. The tunnel sloped upward, and Rothar could feel the faintest draft, a distant promise of fresh air. But the pressure around them grew heavier, the air colder, the faintest whispering beginning to echo off the walls.

It was as if the Bones themselves were alive, guiding them, yet trying to hold them back.

A sharp crack rang out from behind them, and Rothar whirled, his sword raised as he searched for the source. But the sound was followed only by silence, heavy and unnatural. He turned back, urging Leena forward as the whispers grew louder, the words indistinguishable but laced with menace. His heart hammered, each beat a reminder of how close the darkness was pressing.

"Almost there," Leena rasped.

Ahead of them, a faint light gleamed, a crack in the ceiling where the smallest glimmer of dawn reached into the depths. Rothar felt his spirits lift, and he pulled her along, pushing through the pain and exhaustion.

The shadows clawed at them, swirling in agitation as they neared the exit, until, with a final push, they broke through a narrow opening, scrambling up the incline.

Rothar emerged first, his chest heaving as he sucked in the damp, smoky, heavy air of Hollow-Gate's streets. He turned, reaching down to help Leena up, her fingers cold as they gripped his.

They pulled themselves into a crooked alley, and only then did Rothar dare to look back into the dark opening below. For a heartbeat, the shadows shifted, seeming to reach out for them with clawed, grasping hands before sinking back into the depths. Rothar's pulse slowed, but the weight of what they'd escaped lingered, a reminder that the darkness below was far from gone.

CHAPTER 6: THE WEB TIGHTENS

The morning dawned over HollowGate, weak and gray, as if the sun itself could not penetrate the city's endless shadow. Rothar and Leena leaned against the stone wall of the alley, their breath mingling with the cold mist that hung in the air. Each shallow inhale felt like victory, their escape still fresh and raw, yet they knew the danger was far from over.

The thin light filtered down into the narrow alleyways, casting long, shivering shadows across the cobblestones. Rothar scanned their surroundings, every sense heightened, alert to any sign of pursuit. The city's usual sounds—the distant call of a vendor, the clink of metal from a far-off blacksmith's forge—felt muted, ominous, as though the streets themselves were holding their breath.

Leena's hand moved instinctively to her wand, her fingers brushing over its surface as though to reassure herself it was still there. She cast a wary glance at the shadowed entrance to the Bones, then met Rothar's gaze.

"That was too close," she said, her voice strained, the toll of the night weighing heavy in her eyes.

Rothar nodded, his expression grim. "Close doesn't begin to cover it. But we're out, and that's what matters." He took a deep breath, the cool air sharp against his lungs, cutting through the lingering terror that clung to him like smoke.

Leena pulled her cloak tighter around her, casting a look toward the eastern edge of the city where the sun had just broken through the mist. "Whatever we face next," she said quietly, "it's better than what's down there."

Rothar's jaw clenched as he stared down the alley, his hand resting on his sword. "Agreed. But if what's down there follows us up here, Hollow-Gate has more to fear than it knows."

The city's dawn stretched over them, thin and pale, but the two of them stood in its light, resolute, ready to face whatever shadows waited on the surface.

"Ever seen the city this quiet?" Rothar muttered, his eyes sweeping over shuttered stalls and darkened windows. He glimpsed movement—a shadow, the quick flicker of a face disappearing behind a curtain, eyes glinting with suspicion and fear.

"No," Leena replied, her voice low but steady. "But we stirred the pot, and now everyone is waiting to see what floats to the top."

The silence wasn't just an absence of sound; it was a presence, pressing down on them with the weight of a thousand unseen eyes. Rothar's hand drifted to the hilt of his sword, fingers brushing the worn leather grip. HollowGate had always been a city that thrived on noise: the bark of vendors, the clash of metal, the lamentations of the despoiled spilling from taverns. This new quiet felt like an omen, and Rothar didn't like omens.

"But where to go, now?" Leena mumbled to herself. "Maybe we'll go see Talia—"

"Joren," Rothar cut her off, not wanting to see the witch again, and not all-in-all trusting Leena's instincts when it came to magic. "We do this with Joren, this time," Rothar said, doing his best to seem unmovable.

She looked at him, rolled her eyes. She seemed to want to say something, then exhaled. "Fine, your way. The snake."

Back in The Sprawl, they turned down a narrow alley, the walls slick with moss and the air heavy with the smell of rain-soaked stone and refuse. The alley twisted and split, leading them to a hidden entrance that opened into a tavern known only to those who thrived in the spaces between law and shadow. The Black Kettle was dimly lit, its tables populated by mercenaries, informants, and the kind of people whose loyalties could be bought with enough coin. It wasn't like the Iron Stag, where Orrin kept things acceptably civil if not honest, with his strength of character and a well-used cudgel. No. not like that at all.

The low hum of conversation resumed as Rothar and Leena stepped inside, eyes tracking them before flicking back to tankards and whispered deals. Rothar's gaze settled on a man hunched in the far corner, a hood pulled low over his face. The sharp scent of spiced ale and smoke filled the air, mingling with the murmur of voices and the scrape of chairs against the wooden floor. A subtle nod passed between them, the silent recognition of old allies. This was Joren, a former servant of the Silver Eclipse who now traded in secrets like coin. Rothar led Leena to the table, sliding onto the bench opposite their contact.

"Rothar. It's been a while," Joren said, his voice rough and low, like gravel shifting underfoot. His eyes darted to Leena, dark brows lifting slightly. "Bringing company these days, I see."

"Time's changed," Rothar replied, cutting to the chase. "We need information about Velora and any allies she might have kept outside the estate."

Joren's mouth twitched—not quite a smile, but the echo of one. His fingers drummed on the table, a nervous rhythm that betrayed his usual calm. "You're asking dangerous questions, friend. The Eclipse doesn't take kindly to people poking at their secrets."

"We know that already," Leena interjected, leaning forward. The faint scent of the dried herbs she carried drifted between them, sharp and earthy. "We're not asking for favors. We're asking for names."

Joren's eyes flickered, and he sighed, the weight of the request pressing down on the space between them. He reached into his cloak and drew out a scrap of parchment, creased and stained at the edges. "Velora wasn't alone. She had visitors, ones the Eclipse would never acknowledge. There's talk of a group called the Silent Veil. They've been spreading like mold through the cracks of HollowGate, meeting in places even the Eclipse wouldn't venture."

Rothar's brow furrowed as he took the parchment, eyes scanning the spidery, jagged letters and the arcane symbols scrawled around them. The taste of copper stung at the back of his throat, the ghost of a childhood warning his father used to mutter: *Power unseen is power most dangerous.*

"Where do we find them?" Rothar asked, voice flat but urgent.

Joren's eyes glimmered with a mixture of fear and greed. He leaned in, his voice dropping to a near whisper. "They're protected by more than just steel. Magic older than HollowGate itself guards their gatherings."

Leena's expression hardened, a glint in her eyes that reflected both dread and determination. "So, we've heard. We can handle magic."

Joren glanced between them, his unease palpable. "Their meetings are in the catacombs beneath the city. Old places where the skeletons of HollowGate's past rest uneasy. You'll find an entrance in the old temple—"

Before Rothar could process the implications, a crash shattered the quiet tension of their conversation. His head snapped up just as a table overturned, tankards and dice scattering across the floor. A group of masked figures, clad in dark cloaks and bearing the sigil of an eye circled in thorns, surged into the room.

"The Silent Veil, I presume?" Leena breathed.

Chaos erupted. Chairs scraped back as patrons leapt from their seats, tankards clattering to the ground. The glint of knives flashed in the dim light, and voices shouted in panic. Rothar's instincts kicked in, muscles coiling as one of the cultists lunged at him, blade slicing through the air where his neck had been a heartbeat before. He twisted, the movement fluid, and drove his fist into the attacker's ribs, feeling the bone crack under the force.

Leena's voice rang out, sharp and commanding. Her incantation wove through the din, and blue sparks crackled from her fingers, arcing toward another cultist who fell back with a shout, eyes wide as the spell slammed him into a table. The tavern was a storm of sound—the clash of steel, the scrape of boots, and the deep, guttural chants of the cultists that resonated in Rothar's chest like a drumbeat as tavern goers fled for the exits.

"Back door!" Rothar shouted, parrying another blade as he moved toward Leena. She spun away from him, eyes narrowing as she flicked her wrist, her wand clutched in her fingers. It flared, and the cultist in her path stumbled, movements slowing as though trapped in tar.

Rothar's sword met another blade, the clash sending shocks up his arm. The cultist's eyes were wild, pupils blown wide, and his breath came in ragged, rotten-smelling gasps. Rothar pushed forward, forcing the man back with quick, precise strikes. The noise of the fight was deafening, filling his ears with the scrape of steel, the shouts of pain, and the sharp snap of magic. But where was Joren?

"Joren!" Rothar shouted, but the din was too loud, his voice lost in the scuffle. He fought his way through the attackers, trying to see if Joren had made it out. But the cultists pressed in from all sides, and Rothar barely had time to draw breath as he warded off another strike.

Leena ducked beneath a dagger, the blade slicing through her sleeve but missing skin. She muttered another incantation, sending a pulse of air that knocked her attacker off his feet, the crash of his fall swallowed by the cacophony. For a heartbeat, the path to the back door was clear. Rothar didn't waste it. He shoved through, pulling Leena behind him as they stumbled into the narrow alley.

The clamor of the fight became muffled by the sudden press of fog and silence.

Their breaths came in harsh, ragged gasps, mist swirling around them like specters. Rothar tasted blood, the metallic tang sharp on his tongue. The thin trickle of sweat down his back was cold despite the heat of battle that still hummed in his veins. Leena's chest rose and fell rapidly, her eyes darting to the shifting shadows.

"They knew," she said, voice tight with realization. "They were waiting for us."

Rothar's grip on his sword tightened until his knuckles whitened. "Which means we're being watched. Or worse—someone's talking. What about the witch—"

Leena's eyes narrowed, her mind working quickly as she pieced the implications together. She cut him off, before he could voice his thoughts, "No chance," she snapped, leaving no room, no time, for discussion. "This so-called

Silent Veil must have spies in the city, someone high up or well connected—"

"Did Joren make it out?" Rothar gasped, not worrying about bigger things just then. He lost contact with the mercenary in the crush.

Leena shook her head, her face ashen. "I don't know. But we have what we need now, thanks to him."

Rothar took a breath, his jaw clenched. "Then we'll make sure it's not for nothing."

The distant sound of boots striking stone echoed through the fog, growing louder. Rothar's eyes met Leena's, a shared understanding passing between them. Without another word, he led her into the warren of alleys threading beneath the city. The familiar damp stench of the tunnels greeted them, a mix of moss, rot, and old stone. Water dripped in steady beats, echoing through the narrow spaces like a heartbeat.

They moved quickly, the light from the wand casting ghostly shadows on the slick walls. Rothar glanced back, eyes catching the glint of torchlight far behind them, the pursuers moving with relentless purpose. He pushed them harder, muscles aching as they slipped deeper into the maze.

They paused in a small alcove where the sound of dripping water was louder, masking their panting breaths. The glow from Leena's charm was the only light, casting sharp lines across their faces. Rothar wiped the sweat from his brow, the cut on his arm stinging with each pulse of blood. His eyes searched the dark, half-expecting more cultists to emerge from the shadows.

"Joren's information wasn't worth this," he said, the words coming out harsher than he intended. Anger and frustration churned in his gut, fueled by the sting of betrayal and the bite of exhaustion.

Leena's gaze didn't falter, her eyes fierce in the pale light. "It's worth it if it stops what Velora started. If we don't find the Silent Veil's heart, then everything we've done means nothing."

"Easy for you to say," Rothar muttered, his voice thick with bitterness. "You're the one wielding the spells."

Her eyes flashed, a spark of anger igniting in them. "And you're the one cutting us a path through them. We need each other, Rothar. Whether you trust that or not."

The silence that followed was weighted with everything left unsaid. Rothar's jaw tightened, but he gave the smallest nod—a concession, an unspoken agreement. He turned, eyes catching on a symbol carved into the damp stone of the alleyway. It was an eye circled by thorns, its edges worn smooth by years of water and grime. The same emblem on the man's cloak. The same emblem they saw in Velora's apartments.

"They've been here longer than we thought," he said, tracing the sigil with a calloused finger. The cold of the stone seemed to seep into his bones, an echo of something ancient and malevolent.

Leena's gaze followed his, the determination in her eyes hardening. "Then we're closer than we think."

The sound of boots striking stone echoed closer now, their pursuers relentless. Rothar met Leena's eyes, a grim understanding passing between them. "Now, we need to find this temple . . ." she let the words linger.

"Let's move," he said, "I know where it is." He stepped into the dark with Leena at his side. The chill of the city pressed around them, heavy with the weight of secrets and the threat of what lay ahead.

CHAPTER 7: THE CULT'S LAIR

T he abandoned chapel to the merciful god Solentis, a deity once revered, loomed like a forgotten giant on the outskirts of HollowGate, its stone walls cracked and crawling with corrupted ivy that shivered in the morning breeze, its dilapidated and degraded façade a testament to its once great, now lost power. Rothar hissed under his breath. *Solentis waits*, he thought, he hoped.

The stale air inside was tinged with the metallic bite of long-dried blood and mildew. Morning light filtered through shattered stained-glass windows, casting jagged, kaleidoscopic shards of color across the cracked stone floor. Rothar shifted his weight, the familiar pressure of his sword belt digging into his hip, the subtle creak of his leather armor a reminder that silence here was no ally.

Across the room, Leena stood by a weathered altar, fingers tracing the carvings as if they could whisper some forgotten secret to her. "Are you ready for this?" Rothar asked, his voice low and almost swallowed by the chapel's cold silence.

Leena turned, the blue glow of her wand casting an eerie light across her features. Determination hardened her eyes, their pale blue deepening into a stormy shade. "We've come too far to hesitate now."

Rothar's jaw clenched. The tension between them was as tight as a bowstring. The echoes of their last fight still lingered between them, but this morning, the air carried a heavier promise—finality. He nodded, unspeaking, and they moved to the cracked stone floor where an iron ring was set into a trapdoor, half-hidden by debris—just where Joren had said. The scent of mildew and cold earth rose to meet them as they pried it open, revealing a dark maw that seemed to breathe out a chill.

The descent into the catacombs was steep, the slick walls pressing in with damp, cold fingers. Each step down was a plunge into deeper darkness, the wand's weak light barely piercing the shadows. The sound of water dripping somewhere distant echoed through the narrow passage, masking other, subtler noises that hinted at things shifting just out of sight. Rothar's hand never strayed far from his sword, the leather of his gloves creaking as his grip tightened. Every step was a weight pressing into his bones, each echoing drip a reminder of time slipping away.

"Do you hear that?" Leena's whisper cut through the dark, barely more than a breath.

Rothar paused, straining to listen. It was there—low and rhythmic, a pulse beneath the stone that reverberated through his chest. The deeper they moved, the stronger it grew, until it was unmistakable: a chant, carried on the damp air and brushing past his ears like a secret not meant for them.

The corridor widened into a cavernous chamber where the air thickened, laced with the acrid scent of smoke and something metallic. Braziers flickered along the walls, casting restless, shifting light over hooded figures that stood in concentric circles around a raised dais. At its center, a figure, robed in deep red raised their arms, chanting in a language that grated against Rothar's senses, sharp and jagged like the scrape of a blade on stone.

Leena's fingers brushed his arm, grounding him as they slipped behind a crumbling pillar. The cold stone bit into his cheek as he pressed against the pillar to watch. But Rothar ignored it, eyes locked on the ritual unfolding before them. Power gathered in the room, a palpable force that made the hairs on his neck stand up.

"This is it," Leena said, awe and dread entwined in her voice.

Rothar's gaze swept over the room, noting the gaunt faces and fevered eyes of the cultists, each swaying to the rhythmic chant. A metallic glint caught his eye—a dagger, long and thin, held aloft by the figure at the dais. Sigils etched along the blade pulsed faintly, feeding on the energy that crackled in the air.

"This is madness," Rothar said, fingers tightening on the hilt of his sword. "We need to leave. Regroup."

"No." Leena's voice was fierce, her gaze fixed on the ritual. "This is our only chance. If we don't stop them now—"

A sudden shift silenced them both. The chanting paused, hanging in the air like a drawn breath. The figure at the dais spoke no words. But a power, resonant and dark, seemed to issue forth from his cowled face, a silent command that sent a shiver through Rothar's core. The cultists turned as one, their eyes glinting like polished stones beneath their hoods, seeking out the intruders with predatory awareness.

"Move!" Rothar barked, drawing his sword in a swift, practiced motion. The room erupted into chaos as the cultists surged forward, their guttural battle cries reverberating like thunder.

Leena's hand shot up, the wand in her grasp flaring with blue light as she uttered an incantation. A wave of force rippled out, knocking the first row of cultists back. The air thrummed with the aftershock, and Rothar felt the unwelcome sting of magic skitter along his skin. He pushed forward, meeting a cultist's dagger with his blade, the sharp ring of steel echoing in the chamber. The strike bit deep, and the cultist gasped, eyes wide and wild as he fell.

Another cultist lunged, eyes blazing with fanatical fervor. Rothar sidestepped, boots scraping on stone, and brought his sword down in a brutal arc. The clash of metal and bone jarred up his arm, the cultist crumpling at his feet. Before he could catch his breath, another assailant surged forward, his hood falling to reveal a face marked by ritual scars, eyes wide with a mad devotion.

Leena's voice cut through the chaos, her magic crackling like lightning as it seared across the room. The blue energy struck a cluster of cultists, their robes smoldering and cries of pain slicing through the air. The flames from the braziers leaped higher, casting erratic shadows that made the room feel alive, breathing, waiting.

"Leena!" Rothar shouted, slicing down another opponent as he pushed toward her. "We're getting out of here. Now."

She didn't respond, her focus locked on the dais where the leader stood unmoving amidst the chaos. The figure's lips curled into a thin smile, eyes closed as if savoring the energy in the room. The chanting shifted, resonating like a drumbeat against Rothar's chest.

A burst of light erupted from the dais, jagged and bright, arcing toward Leena. She raised her arms, and the impact sent her flying backward, her body slamming into a pillar with a bone-jarring thud. Rothar's heart lurched as he fought his way to her, muscles straining as the metallic scent of blood filled his nostrils.

"Leena!" he shouted, dropping to one knee beside her, hands gripping her shoulders. Her lashes fluttered, eyes unfocused but defiant when they met his.

"We can't let them finish," she gasped, each word labored and raw. "If they do—"

A roar cut her off, a cry from the dais as the leader raised the dagger high, the sigils glowing like embers. The cultists formed a barrier, bodies braced as if prepared to die for whatever dark power was being summoned.

A deep, resonating hum filled the chamber, the stones underfoot vibrating as if the room itself were alive. Rothar felt it through his boots, through the hilt of his sword—a sound that settled in his chest, deep and primal.

"Rothar, we need to disrupt the circle," Leena said, struggling to stand, her hands trembling but steady. The determination in her eyes made something twist in his chest, an unbidden wave of respect and fear.

He nodded once. "We'll do it together."

They moved in tandem, Rothar's sword flashing in precise arcs as he cut through the tide of cultists. Each strike met resistance, pushing him to the edge of his strength. Leena's magic wove between their movements as she waved her deadly wand from one enemy to the next, a dance of fire and shadow. The braziers flickered wildly, flames stretching as if reaching for the ceiling.

Finally, they broke through, standing at the base of the dais. The leader's eyes snapped open, black as midnight, locking onto them with a gaze that burned with malice and a hint of triumph.

"You're too late," the leader rasped, his voice cutting through the din with razor precision.

Leena's fingers curled, a chant spilling from her lips as Rothar lunged forward, sword poised to strike. The cult leader moved with the sudden grace of a serpent, the dagger slashing toward Rothar's chest. He twisted, the blade grazing his side and cutting through his mail as though it were mere cotton or wool and igniting a flare of pain that coursed through him like fire.

The sigils on the dagger flared, and a pulse of dark energy surged outward, knocking both Rothar and Leena back. Rothar's vision blurred, the room spinning as he struggled to keep his footing. The roar of the battle dulled, replaced by a high-pitched ring in his ears. He blinked hard, forcing his focus back as Leena's chant reached a fevered pitch, the air around her vibrating with power.

A final, searing light burst from her wand, slamming into the cult leader with a force that shattered the nearest brazier, sending shards of hot metal skittering across the stone. The leader's scream was thin, ragged, and cut short as he crumpled, the dagger slipping from his grasp and clattering to the floor.

The cultists stilled, their movements frozen, eyes staring blankly as the force that had driven them dissipated like smoke. The room felt as though it exhaled around them, a deep, resounding silence settling over the chamber.

Rothar staggered, one hand pressed to the burning wound at his side, the other reaching for Leena. She stood, trembling but unbroken, eyes locked on the fallen leader. The sigils etched into the stone floor glowed faintly, a final pulse of light before fading.

"It's not over," she whispered, a shiver running down her spine.

Rothar nodded, the ache in his body dwarfed by the knowledge of what they'd just unleashed—and what they still faced. He met her eyes, determination mirrored in his own. "Then we finish this."

Side by side, they turned toward the dark passage that would take them back to HollowGate's surface, where the next battle awaited in the shadowed corners of the city.

CHAPTER 8: THE RIFT

They emerged from the catacombs into the rain-slicked streets of HollowGate. Dawn's pale light pressed down like a weary sigh, its weak glow barely enough to chase the shadows from the alleys. The city, usually a cacophony of vendors' shouts, the clash of metal, and the rhythmic clatter of hooves, was unnervingly silent. Rain pattered in steady rivulets from rooftops, forming thin, dark streams along the cracked cobblestones. The air was thick with the metallic tang of rain and the faint, acrid scent of smoke.

Rothar's side burned where the cult leader's dagger had sliced him, the wound seeping blood that mixed with the rain, tracing crimson streaks down his tunic. Each step sent a fresh spike of pain through him, but he bit back the groan that threatened to escape. His eyes darted to Leena, who walked with her shoulders rigid, eyes locked forward and jaw set. The glow of her wand had faded, and exhaustion was etched in the dark smudges beneath her eyes.

"Can you make it?" Leena's voice was sharp and practical. She looked to him now, concern buried beneath layers of resolve.

Rothar nodded, though his jaw clenched against the pain. "We need to get back. We're exposed out here."

They cut through narrow alleys, their steps echoing off the damp stone walls that loomed close on either side. The city felt more alive than it should, an unseen presence slithering along the periphery of their awareness. Every shadow seemed to shift, every whisper of wind sounded like a murmur just out of reach. Rothar's instincts screamed that they were being watched, but nothing stirred in the gloom except the steady patter of rain.

The smell of damp earth and mildew thickened as they turned a corner, splashing through puddles that reflected fractured slices of the storm-heavy sky. A door loomed ahead, half-hidden by the mist. Rothar's fingers fumbled with the latch, slick with blood and rain, before it clicked open. They slipped inside, the wooden barrier groaning shut behind them. The air within was stale, redolent of old smoke and oil, tinged with the faint, ghostly aroma of charred herbs.

Rothar dropped onto a bench, its wood creaking beneath his weight. His wound throbbed, each heartbeat sending fresh, fiery pulses of pain through his side. He wiped the rain and sweat from his face with a rough hand, tasting blood on his cracked lips. His vision wavered, the edges narrowing to a tunnel as the room seemed to spin.

Leena moved quickly, lighting the lamp with hands that trembled only slightly. The flame sputtered and flared, casting jittery shadows that crawled up the walls and across the scattered maps, empty vials, and scraps of parchment that littered the table. She rummaged through her satchel, pulling out gauze and a small glass bottle filled with a pungent, greenish liquid.

"Hold still," she commanded, not waiting for him to respond before pressing a cloth soaked with the bitter liquid to his wound. Rothar grunted, the sting biting deep, eating into his skin. He focused on a crack in the ceiling, letting the pain anchor him to consciousness.

"I can't believe you pushed that far," he said through gritted teeth, eyes snapping open to meet hers. "You almost—"

Leena's expression turned glacial, her jaw clenched to keep the fatigue from breaking her resolve. "I did what had to be done. We're alive, aren't we?"

"Barely," Rothar shot back, pushing her hand away once she finished. He sat up, the room steadying around him, though his heart still raced. "Every time you use that power, I wonder if it's you or whatever darkness you're pulling from."

A thick, stifling silence fell between them. The rain drummed against the window, filling the void where words should have been. Leena turned her back, leaning over the table where she spread out the tattered pages they'd recovered from the catacombs. The edges were browned with age, the ink faded but legible, whispering of rituals, convergences, and warnings long ignored.

"I felt it," she admitted, voice low and strained, as though the confession was a weight pressing on her. "When I channeled that last spell, it was there—like a breath against my neck. The Whispering One is closer than we think."

A chill rippled through Rothar's gut. He had heard stories of those who pushed too far, who let magic take root in their bones and feed on their soul until they became something else. Watching Leena now, silhouetted in the lamp's glow, he wondered if she was already on that edge.

"You're not like them," he said finally, the gruffness in his voice failing to mask the worry beneath. "But you need to pull back before—"

"Before what?" She turned, eyes flaring with an intensity that silenced him. "Before I end up like Velora? Or worse, consumed by whatever she awakened? You think I don't know the risks? We're running out of time, Rothar. If I don't use everything I have, we won't survive what's coming."

Her words, brittle with fear and resolve, lodged in his chest like a stone. Rothar's fingers flexed around the hilt of his sword, the familiar cool leather grounding him amid the turmoil.

A sharp knock echoed through the room, deliberate and precise. Rothar's body tensed, his blade halfway out of its scabbard before Leena raised a hand, a silent warning. The knock came again—three quick raps followed by a pause. A contact's signal.

Leena moved to the door, peering through the slats. The tension crackled between them until she opened the door just enough to let in a slim figure wrapped in a soaked cloak. The man's face was drawn tight with cold, eyes darting nervously as he slipped inside. The scent of wet wool filled the room, mingling with the tang of lamp oil and sweat.

"They're moving," the man said, voice barely above a rasp. "The cult. They're gathering at the old well beneath the city, the one that touches the deep channels."

Rothar's pulse quickened. The well was more than just a forgotten landmark; it was a relic from when HollowGate was still new, a place whispered to be where the boundaries between realms thinned. If the cult was planning to use it . . .

"Shadows have been seen in the alleys, speaking in voices that don't match the lips moving," the contact continued, eyes wide with fear. "The city's on edge. Whatever they're planning, it's close."

Leena's hand shook as she pulled a parchment closer, its ink smudged from the damp. The notes matched what she had deciphered in the catacombs—an incantation, fragmented but powerful, pointing to the well as a focal point.

Rothar met her gaze, a silent conversation passing between them. There was no room left for hesitation or doubt, only the stark understanding that they had to act.

"Get back to your place and stay out of sight," Rothar said, his tone brooking no argument. The man nodded, casting a final, nervous glance over his shoulder before disappearing into the rain.

Leena's eyes shone with a mix of determination and something darker. "We need to stop them before they open that gateway."

Rothar sheathed his sword, the sound a sharp promise in the silence. "To the end, then."

They stepped into the night, the rain a steady hiss that soaked through their cloaks and chilled their skin to the bone. The streets lay shrouded in a twilight gloom, the usual glow of lamps and chatter of voices replaced by an uneasy stillness. Rothar's boots splashed in puddles that mirrored fractured glimpses of the sky, streaked with bruised clouds.

The old well lay in the heart of the Sprawl, where the city's oldest district rotted and decayed, where buildings sagged with age and ivy crawled like veins across their facades. Even to the degenerated Sprawl, it seemed depraved and forgotten by anyone whose soul remained intact. The closer they got, the more the air seemed to vibrate with a low, pulsing hum that set Rothar's teeth on edge. Leena's breath came in short, controlled bursts, the faint light of her wand barely cutting through the thickening mist.

They rounded a last corner, stopping short as the well came into view. Hooded figures—more of the damnable cultists—encircled it, their robes fluttering in an unseen wind. Candles flickered at their feet, flames dancing with unnatural life. At the well's edge, a figure in deep red, his robe more ornate than the others—threads of twisting gold and silver script wrapping about his cowl and glittering at his wrists—raised his arms, voice rising in a chant that grated on Rothar's senses, reverberating with a sound both ancient and wrong. Along the top of the will, the cultists had inked that same twisted script they'd seen in Velora's rooms. It pulsed and glowed with angry, violet energy.

Leena's fingers twitched with the beginnings of a spell, eyes narrowing. Rothar held up a hand, a silent plea for patience.

"Wait for my signal," he whispered.

The chant swelled, thickening the air as if it were suffused with smoke. Rothar felt it pressing against his skin, filling his lungs like a noxious fog. The leader's voice boomed, and the sigils around the well flared, bleeding light into the rain-soaked mist.

"Now," Rothar said, charging forward with a battle cry that split the night. His blade met flesh, the first cultist crumpling with a strangled gasp. Leena's incantation rang out, sharp and fierce, a burst of blue light scattering two figures like leaves in a storm.

The battle descended into chaos.

Rothar's world became a blur of motion and pain, the clash of steel and the wet thud of bodies hitting stone filling the air. Blood sprayed, hot and coppery, across his face as he parried a thrust and drove his sword into the gap beneath a cultist's hood. The man's eyes rolled white before he collapsed, a sickening gurgle his last sound. The acrid stench of sweat, blood, and iron mingled with the relentless downpour that hissed as it struck the cobblestones.

Leena's voice cut through the din, clear and sharp, her spell-casting desperate and unyielding. Each incantation sent shivers of energy crackling through the rain, knocking back attackers who lunged for her with frenzied, unblinking eyes. One cultist spun toward Rothar, dagger gleaming, her face contorted in an expression that was both human and not. Rothar dodged, boots skidding on the slick stone, and brought his blade up in a vicious arc that caught the cultist across the chest. The body slumped, lifeless, into the muddy puddle at his feet.

"Rothar, they're drawing power from the well!" Leena shouted, her voice raw with exertion. The ground beneath their feet trembled as if the earth itself were trying to recoil from the ritual's dark energy. The well's light had grown, a pulsing pillar that clawed at the storm clouds, twisting the rain into an oily, iridescent curtain.

Rothar's muscles burned as he swung again and again, each strike taking him closer to the heart of the circle. The cult leader stood at the well's edge, his chant growing deeper, more resonant, resonating in Rothar's chest like a war drum. The sigils on the ground glowed brighter, their light bleeding up into the surrounding mist and painting the scene in a sickly, otherworldly hue.

Out of the corner of his eye, Rothar saw Leena moving closer to the well. Her face was pale, lips moving in frantic whispers as she carved symbols in the air, the wand in her hand blazing with blue fire. A thin line of blood traced from her nose, mixing with the rain as she poured everything she had into disrupting the ritual.

The chanting rose to a crescendo, and with a swift, savage motion, the high priest—or whatever he was—plunged the dagger into the well's surface. The energy rippled outward in a shockwave that sent Rothar sprawling, the impact searing through his already battered body. He landed hard, the rough stone tearing at his skin, the metallic taste of blood flooding his mouth. Around them, cracks split the ground, glowing with the same eerie light as the sigils. The vibrations threatened to shatter bone and splinter the world apart.

"Leena!" Rothar roared, pushing himself up despite the pain roaring through his side. His vision swam, dark edges threatening to close in, but he forced himself to focus. He saw Leena, barely standing, eyes wide with terror but lit with unrelenting determination.

"We have to break the circle!" she screamed, her voice almost lost in the howling wind and booming chant. The air around her crackled as she raised her free hand, the wand in the other flickering dangerously.

Rothar lunged into the fray, cutting through the last line of cultists who moved with a wild, erratic speed that defied logic. Blood spattered as his sword met flesh, his arm trembling with exhaustion. Each movement sent sharp bolts of agony through his side, but he ignored it, driven by the singular purpose of reaching the well.

The unholy priest spun to face Leena, eyes glittering with dark power as he raised a hand, black energy swirling into a deadly orb between his fingers. Rothar saw it happen in a blink, his mind screaming out the warning. He charged, boots pounding on stone, and barreled into the leader just as the spell discharged. The dark energy shot wide, striking a nearby cultist who fell with a bone-chilling scream. Rothar and the leader tumbled to the ground, grappling in a vicious struggle, daggers and fists colliding in a blur of movement.

"Leena!" Rothar yelled as he fought, his breath ragged. She was at the well's edge now, pressing her hand against the stone and muttering the final, desperate words of an incantation that seemed to pull the air from the surrounding square. The sigils flared once, twice, before the glow began to sputter and die. The candles flickered, their flames sputtering out one by one as Leena's magic washed over them.

A scream tore from the cult leader's throat, filled with fury and desperation as the light around the well extinguished, leaving only the thin, wavering light of the storm. Rothar seized the moment, slamming his sword into the leader's chest with a final, resounding strike. The man's eyes met his, wide and disbelieving, before the light in them went dark. The body crumpled, lifeless, onto the rain-slick stone, leaving nothing but an eerie silence.

Rothar staggered back, barely keeping to his feet, while the rain began to fall in steady, quiet drips, washing away the blood from the cold stone around the well.

For a moment, that silence reigned. Then sound began to return—at first, the storm's roar seemed distant, a muted backdrop to the gasps and groans of the wounded. His chest heaved, his hand pressed against his side as he stumbled toward Leena. She swayed on her feet, eyes fluttering shut as the last of her strength drained away, for the second time in as many days—and for the last time, he foolishly swore to himself, even as he knew it was a lie. And again, as her fingers brushed over the evil sigils carved into the stone.

"It's over," he murmured, though the words felt more hollow than victorious. He tightened his hold on her, trying to convince himself it was true.

Leena's eyes cracked open, a faint gleam of doubt flickering within them. "Over ... or ... ?" She let her voice trail off, her gaze lingering on the well, the dark water within swirling in ways that defied the quiet air around them.

A shuddering pulse seemed to echo from the depths, a barely perceptible ripple. Rothar tensed, feeling the prickle of unease travel up his spine.

"We should leave," he said, but his words barely felt strong enough to break the grip of whatever still lingered, unseen, within the shadows cast by the ancient well. As he glanced one last time at the stone, something dark and shifting seemed to glint at the bottom.

Together, they turned and began to retreat, the silence pressing around them heavier with every step, the stillness leaving one final, unshakable question: was it truly over?

CHAPTER 9: FACING THE WHISPERING ONE

The well seemed to pulse faintly behind them, its dark energy reaching into the chill air. Rothar's legs felt like lead, exhaustion clawing at his bones, but an insistent hum made him pause. He turned slowly, his instincts screaming, and pulled Leena back beside him as a shadow began to ripple from the depths. It rose like smoke, dark and thick, curling with the unnatural grace of something alive. The whispers began again, threading through the air like poisoned silk, twisting into thoughts he couldn't hold onto.

"It isn't done," Rothar murmured, his voice barely audible over the sound of the well. Beside him, Leena turned, her pale face streaked with rain and wide with horror. From the depths of the well, the shifting darkness began to take shape, twisting into a form both monstrous and horrifyingly familiar.

The air thickened, pressing down on them like a suffocating weight as the shadow loomed larger, its presence suffused with an unbearable cold. Rothar's breath hitched as the figure stretched upward, its limbs flowing like liquid, its form defying logic and comprehension. And then—horribly—he saw it: a face at the heart of the swirling nightmare, fractured and shifting but unmistakable.

Velora.

Her beauty lingered, but it was grotesquely transformed, her once-luminous eyes now voids that burned with an otherworldly malice. Her features flickered in and out of focus, caught between human and inhuman, as if the essence of her humanity had been devoured and corrupted by the very magic she had sought to control.

Leena staggered, her hand gripping Rothar's arm as though to anchor herself. "Velora?" she whispered, disbelief and fear breaking through her voice.

The apparition's head twisted toward her, the motion jerky and unnatural, and Velora's ruined visage grinned, splitting her face into something far too wide, her teeth sharp as daggers. When she spoke, her voice was layered—a discordant symphony of the woman she had been and the monstrosity she had become.

"Leena," it crooned, mockingly tender. "I see you. Feel you. You are like me."

The sound was enough to send a shudder down Rothar's spine. His grip tightened on his sword, though his fingers felt numb against the hilt. "It's not her," he growled, forcing the words through gritted teeth. "Not anymore."

The figure laughed, the sound stretching impossibly, echoing as though it came from the deepest recesses of the well. The shadows coiled around her, flowing into her shape, and the form of the Whispering One grew, tendrils of darkness sprouting like living roots. Faces flickered across the tendrils—twisted, desperate, and fleeting—while whispers poured forth, cutting at the edges of their sanity.

Rothar felt the voices burrow into his thoughts, dragging up memories he had buried: the screams of comrades left behind, the weight of failure, the cold certainty of his own mortality. The whispers spoke in familiar tones, twisting loved ones' voices into taunts. You will fail . . . You will be consumed.

Beside him, Leena raised her charm, the blue light flickering unsteadily as if the entity's presence sapped its strength. Her lips moved in a ragged incantation, but the force of the words faltered. Her wide eyes stayed locked on Velora's face, horror etched into her features.

"Don't look at it!" Rothar barked, snapping her out of her trance. "Stay with me!"

Leena's head jerked toward him, her hand trembling as she clenched the charm tighter. "I—I can't. It's her, Rothar. It's Velora."

"It was her," Rothar said harshly, forcing her to meet his eyes. "You saw what she was doing. This thing—whatever it is—it's not her anymore."

The shadow took a step forward, its monstrous form shifting as Velora's face twisted with fury. Her voice, mocking and cruel, reverberated through the courtyard. "Rothar," she hissed, her tone dripping with venom. "You cannot save her. You cannot save yourself."

The weight of her words struck him, the tendrils of shadow curling closer, whispering his failures back to him. He staggered as images of fire and ruin filled his mind—visions of Leena falling, consumed by the same magic that had claimed Velora. His grip on his sword faltered, and the blade dipped.

"Fight it, Rothar!" Leena's voice cut through the haze, her magic flaring brighter. The blue light pushed the shadows back slightly, but the effort drained her. She swayed on her feet, gasping as the oppressive power pressed down on them again.

The Whispering One recoiled, but only for a moment. Velora's visage twisted into something monstrous, her beauty warped into jagged lines and sharp edges. The tendrils surged forward, slamming into Leena's barrier and sending her stumbling back. Rothar caught her before she fell, his hand steadying her as she gritted her teeth against the onslaught.

"You cannot resist," the Whispering One intoned, Velora's voice now hollow and echoing. "You will join me, as she did."

"No!" Leena screamed, her voice raw and defiant. The light from her charm blazed, a flare of hope in the suffocating darkness. She threw her arm forward, a wave of magic surging from her hand. It collided with the Whispering One, causing its form to shudder, Velora's face flickering with pain before the shadow recoiled.

The entity screeched, the sound clawing at their ears as it twisted, tendrils lashing out wildly. Rothar ducked beneath one, his blade cutting through another, though it seemed to reform as quickly as it was severed. The cold seeped into his bones, slowing his movements, but he forced himself forward, each step an act of will.

"Whatever it takes," Leena murmured, the words half to herself as she pushed her magic to its limits. Her face was pale, sweat dripping down her brow as she fought to hold the Whispering One at bay.

The entity shifted, its tendrils coiling tighter, drawing the shadows inward. Velora's face loomed larger, her voice softer now, almost tender. "Leena," she whispered, and for a moment, her tone was the same as it had been in life. "You know what power feels like. Why deny it? Let it in."

Leena hesitated, her hand faltering as the words sank in. Rothar saw the moment of doubt and grabbed her shoulder, shaking her hard. "Don't listen to it! It's lying!"

Velora's face twisted, her grin sharp and cruel. "He doesn't understand. But you do."

Leena's grip on her charm tightened, her eyes narrowing as she shoved the doubt aside. "You're right," she said, her voice cold. "I do understand." She raised her hand, the blue light flaring brighter than ever. "And that's why you don't scare me."

The spell surged forward, slamming into the Whispering One with a force that shattered the courtyard's stillness. The shadow writhed, its tendrils retreating as Velora's face contorted, her scream tearing through the air. Rothar seized the moment, his sword cutting through the heart of the entity's form. The blade struck true, and the Whispering One shuddered violently, its shadow splitting and dissolving into the night.

Velora's face lingered for a moment in the dissipating mist, her expression almost peaceful, before vanishing entirely.

The courtyard fell into an eerie silence, the echoes of the Whispering One's scream fading into the night. Rothar pulled his sword free from the dissipating shadow, his breath heaving in ragged gasps. Around them, the surviving cultists fled like vermin, their minds too shattered to put up further resistance.

Leena staggered toward the edge of the well, her charm flickering faintly against her chest. "Rothar," she called weakly, her voice trembling. "There's something . . ."

He followed her gaze to the center of the well, where the shattered sigils still pulsed faintly with a cold, sickly light. From the ruins of Velora's magic, something gleamed—a crescent-shaped medallion, black as night, resting in the center of the broken stones.

Rothar's stomach churned. "Leave it," he growled, the edge of command in his voice. "That thing—whatever it is—it's not worth it."

But Leena was already reaching for it, her fingers brushing the cold surface of the medallion. She flinched at the contact, as though it had burned her, but her expression remained resolute. "We can't leave this here," she said, her voice quiet but firm. "If we don't take it, someone else will."

Rothar stepped forward, his sword still drawn, and glared at the object. The faint runes on its surface glowed in response, filling the air with a faint hum that made his skin crawl. "And who's to say taking it won't just bring more of this madness?"

Leena held his gaze, her eyes shadowed with exhaustion but unyielding. "I'll take care of it."

He clenched his jaw, his grip on the sword tightening. "That's what Velora probably said too."

"I'm not Velora," she snapped, tucking the medallion into her satchel. "And you'll just have to trust me. Besides this goes to Talia. The payment she requested."

Rothar's scowl deepened, but he didn't argue. As they turned to leave, he muttered under his breath, "I don't trust anyone with something that dark."

Together, they turned toward the city, their steps heavy with the weight of what they'd survived, and what they'd lost.

CHAPTER 10: AFTERMATH AND NEW PATHS

Morning broke over HollowGate like a tentative promise, pale gray light washing over rain-soaked streets that gleamed like polished stone. It was still HollowGate—dim and dark—but the storm had passed, leaving behind the earthy scent of wet ground and the faint, acrid trace of smoke from shattered lanterns and the industrial furnaces already sputtering in the Iron District. Rothar stood by the narrow window of their lair, watching as life—such as it was in this grim place—began to seep back into the city.

Vendors emerged from hidden corners, re-assembling their stalls with wary glances over their shoulders. City guards patrolled in pairs, their hands hovering near their weapons, eyes scanning the streets as though expecting another disaster to rise from the shadows.

Behind him, Leena lay motionless on the makeshift cot, her chest rising and falling in shallow breaths. The bluish tint had faded from her lips, replaced by a fragile flush of color. Her charm, cracked and dulled from the night's ordeal, rested against her collarbone like a badge of survival. The deadly wand she wielded with such practiced ease lay silent on the night table, an unspoken reminder of how close they had come to losing themselves. Rothar's fingers twitched at the memory of that desperate fight—the shadowy blades, the dark whispers that still lingered at the edges of his thoughts.

Watching Leena wield that much magic had stirred something in Rothar, something uneasy. He'd seen the way it had drained her, the toll it had taken—and the way her eyes lingered on the medallion she'd taken from the well. Magic had a way of warping people, of twisting ambition into obsession. Velora had been proof of that.

Leena stirred, breaking the fragile silence. Her eyes fluttered open, revealing that deep, shadowed blue, now older and carrying the weight of something neither of them would admit aloud.

He pushed his dark thoughts away. "Back with me?" Rothar asked, his voice rougher than he intended, barely masking the relief swelling in his chest.

Leena's lips curved into a faint smile, wry but tired. "Barely," she rasped, her voice carrying the strain of exhaustion. She pushed herself up on one elbow, wincing as pain lanced through her side. Between them, silence pulsed, thick with the echoes of everything they'd faced and left unspoken.

Rothar crossed the room and sat at the edge of the cot. He reached for a cloth and dabbed gently at the dried blood crusting her temple. His touch was careful, almost reverent. "You almost didn't come back," he muttered, the words slipping out before he could stop them.

"I know." Leena's gaze drifted, unfocused, as if the whispers still clung to the shadows of the room. "It was close. The power—it called to me. It promised everything if I just . . . let go."

"But you didn't," Rothar said firmly, his voice edged with a fierceness he didn't bother to hide. "You're stronger than that."

Leena's throat worked against a tide of emotion. "I'm still here. For now." Her voice wavered as her eyes shut briefly, as though willing away the memory of the all-consuming darkness.

Rothar looked at her, his jaw tightening. "You know what that power does. You saw it in Velora. It's not a tool—it's a leash, waiting to choke the life out of anyone who thinks they can control it."

Leena opened her eyes and met his gaze, the spark of defiance cutting through her fatigue. "Maybe I'm not like Velora. Maybe I can control it." She gestured to the cracked charm at her neck. "I've learned to walk that edge. I know where it leads."

Rothar shook his head, his expression hardening. "It leads to ashes, Leena. You don't walk that edge without falling. I'll make sure you don't get the chance."

Her smile turned sharper, more self-assured, though it didn't quite reach her eyes. "Rothar the savior, always ready to protect me from myself. I can take care of it—and you know it."

He didn't respond. There was no point arguing with her when she wore that look of defiance, but the weight of his resolve was heavy in the silence between them. He would protect her—whatever it took, even from herself.

The conversation dissolved into a steady rhythm of rainwater dripping from the eaves, the quiet broken only by a sharp knock at the door. Rothar's hand flew to the hilt of his sword as he shot Leena a look. She nodded, shifting to sit up as he moved to the door, cracking it open.

A wiry youth stood in the drizzle, his cloak sodden and eyes wide with urgency. Rothar recognized him as one of the city's messengers.

"The Silver Eclipse sends word," the boy said, his voice trembling under the weight of the news he carried. "They demand your presence before nightfall. They want to know how you succeeded where so many failed."

Rothar's jaw worked, and he nodded curtly. The boy darted away, his feet splashing through the puddles that speckled the cobblestones.

Leena let out a breath, her chuckle carrying a hollow edge. "The Eclipse. Always ready to show up after the mess is cleaned."

Rothar's lips twisted into a dry semblance of a smile. "We need to go," he said, resigned. His gaze softened as it flicked back to her, noting the weariness etched into her face. "But first, you rest."

For once, she didn't argue. She lay back with a faint, trusting smile and closed her eyes. Rothar returned to his vigil by the window, watching as HollowGate exhaled, shedding the remnants of the night's terror. The city bore its scars, but it was alive. So were they.

By the time the sun hung high in the sky, Rothar and Leena were making their way through the streets. Afternoon light sliced through the dissipating mist, illuminating faces peeking cautiously from behind shutters. Whispers followed them as they passed, awe mingled with disbelief at the pair who had emerged victorious from the depths of darkness. But the city didn't know—couldn't know—what had been endured. To HollowGate, it was just another shadow defeated, another tale to add to its grim legends.

Rothar's hand rested lightly on his sword hilt, his gait steady but watchful. Beside him, Leena moved with her usual fluid grace, her sharp blue eyes scanning the crowd for signs of danger. The bond between them, tempered by the fires of the past night, was an unspoken truth neither dared address.

The Tower loomed ahead, its gray stone a monolith against the crimson-hued horizon. Guards flanked the entrance, their polished armor bearing the scars of countless battles. One stepped forward, a veteran with a scar running ear to jaw. His sharp gaze swept over Rothar and Leena before he nodded and stepped aside.

Inside, the air was heavy with the scent of old parchment and melted wax. The chamber's shadows flickered with the light of tall candles, their wavering glow reflecting off the eyes of the gathered councilors. They sat robed and still, their faces a mosaic of suspicion, curiosity, and barely concealed relief. At the head of the table was Captain Tallis, his condescending smirk both infuriating and predictable.

"You succeeded," Tallis said, his tone teetering between impressed and patronizing. "How did you manage it?"

Rothar began to speak, but Leena stepped forward, her commanding presence cutting through the room like a blade. "We faced the heart of the Whispering One's power," she said, her voice steady and unyielding. "We sealed it, but the scars it leaves behind are deep. Don't fool yourselves into thinking it's over."

Tallis' smirk faltered, and whispers rippled through the councilors. A younger member leaned forward, his face hidden beneath the shadow of his hood, but his eyes gleamed with entitlement. "And if it returns? Will you be here when we need you again?"

Rothar glanced at Leena, their shared answer unspoken but certain.

"We'll be here," Rothar said, his voice low but firm. "But not for you. For HollowGate."

As they stepped back into the rain-washed streets of HollowGate, Rothar's thoughts churned. He clenched his fists, feeling the familiar anger rising at the memory of Tallis' smug smirk. The Silver Eclipse—those bastards had known what Velora was doing, had bankrolled it, and then sent him and Leena into the fire when it went wrong. He could still hear Tallis' voice, smooth and condescending, as though they'd done the council a favor rather than cleaning up their mess.

His gaze shifted to Leena, who walked beside him in silence. He imagined he could see the faint outline of the artifact's shape bulged beneath her satchel, and Rothar's stomach twisted. All that was there was coin now. He knew she'd already taken the cursed thing to Talira. She tried to sneak out when he was resting. But, she knew him better than that—at least she should have. Rothar didn't miss much.

"You shouldn't have given that thing to Talira," he said abruptly, the words sharper than he'd intended.

Leena didn't look at him. "She's the only one who can keep it safe. Better her than the Eclipse."

"Better no one," Rothar snapped. "Things like that don't stay 'safe.' They twist people—Velora was proof of that. You think Talira's immune?"

Leena stopped, turning to face him. "And what would you have done? Buried it? Left it for some scavenger to dig up? Besides we promised her payment. We didn't have a choice, Rothar."

His jaw clenched, the tension radiating through him like a coiled spring. "There's always a choice."

She stepped closer, her voice soft but unyielding. "And I made mine."

Rothar didn't reply, his gaze drifting to the horizon. The city's skyline was bathed in the gold and crimson light of the setting sun, but all he could see were the shadows creeping at its edges. Rothar and Leena walked in silence, the weight of survival settling on their shoulders like a shared burden.

At the edge of the district, Rothar paused, his gaze sweeping over the jagged skyline. The city was battered but alive, its heart beating beneath the scars.

"Do you think it's truly over?" Leena asked softly, her voice carrying a note of doubt.

Rothar's mouth curved into a faint, knowing smile. "No. But we've bought ourselves time."

Leena's lips quirked into a tired grin. "Time to heal. Time to prepare."

"Time to find another job, again—after we spend some of that coin," Rothar said, his voice carrying the steely resolve of a man who wouldn't let her—or himself—fall to the darkness.

She looped her arm through his, leaning into him ever so slightly. "Together, then."

The last light of day slipped below the horizon, leaving HollowGate in expectant twilight. Rothar knew that in this city, shadows were always waiting. Whatever came next, they would face it side by side.